SO-AXW-801

Mountain Memories I

BY GRANVILLE A. DEITZ

Copyright   1981

Dennis Deitz

Seventh Printing

Mountain Memories Books
216 Southerland Drive
South Charleston, WV 25303

Contents

THIS SHORT STORY IS AN EXCERPT FROM
THE FLOOD AND THE BLOOD

MOUNTAIN MEMORIES SELECTIONS...

MOUNTAIN MEMORIES SERIES	*$5.95*
THE SEARCH FOR EMILY	*$6.95*
GHOST STORIES	*$7.95*
THE FLOOD AND THE BLOOD	*$20.00*

ORDER FROM:

DENNIS DEITZ
MOUNTAIN MEMORIES BOOKS
216 SUTHERLAND DRIVE
SOUTH CHARLESTON, WV 25303

INTRODUCTION

Once proudly known as the "little Switzerland of America," the State of West Virginia has in recent years become a popular symbol to many of depressed Appalachia, visualized as a hillbilly ghetto, a pocket of grovelling poverty and cultural disadvantage. This image persists in spite of the fact that West Virginia ranks third among the twelve states comprising the southeastern United States in per capita income and first in wage scale for manufacturing and production. Yet heaven only knows how many times the name of our state has been compassionately invoked in pork barrel bills to subsidize poverty.

This little book was inspired by the nagging fear that amid all this morbidity about Appalachia we might lose sight of our proud and immensely colorful forbears. The people who settled these mountains braved nature and savage, and they gave birth to a fascinating breed of mountaineers who were fiercely self-sufficient and chucked full of humor and originality in language and customs. In this book I have tried to preserve for that species of mankind who cherish humor and hillbillies the robust vintage of mountain life. Many of these stories have been handed down to me by more gifted storytellers than myself, but I will vouch for their authenticity because these mountains where they happened are still standing as monuments to these events.

For years some of my friends to whom I have related these stories have urged me to commit them to writing, hoping, I suspect, that it would occupy me. As my experience as a man of letters has been pretty much limited over the years to an occasional indignant note to my congressman, I beg the reader's indulgence of my considerable limitations as an author.

I will try to do as the farmer's cow of which the farmer boasted when asked how much butter fat she gave:

"Oh, she's a good cow. She gives all she's got."

When I finished with the body of the book, I was faced with the problem of getting someone to write an introduction. Every book is supposed to be better if some prominent person writes the preface or some sort of introduction and the more notable the better. My problem was, I didn't know many illustrious figures; and the few reputables with whom I was acquainted were reluctant to stick their necks out on so doubtful a project as mine. There was Jim Comstock, for instance, editor of *"The Hillbilly"* and a well-known authority on mountain lore, who expressed his reluctance this way:

"With our dwindling population, Granville, there are soon going to be more hillbilly writers than readers, so I don't see any future in promoting competition, no matter how lousy his product."

Next I thought of Pearl Buck. She would have been a natural, a native of the hills, born in a county adjacent to mine and her world-famous and all that. But then I got to thinking that she wouldn't write about anything not Chinese or Oriental and unless I changed my name to Ming Ho or Chang Lee or something like that, I wouldn't get anywhere with her. As I was about to exhaust my list of logical suspects to do me an introduction, I lapsed into frustrated despair. My wife began to inquire about whatever it was that was making me more impossible than usual and I broke down and confessed that I couldn't find a good candidate to launch my book and that a book without an introducer was about as crippled as a wagon without a wheel.

My wife solved that problem in nothing flat—as usual. Said she:

"Why don't you introduce the writer. You know him better than Jim Comstock or anyone else. In fact, half your life has been spent admiring him in the mirror and you've certainly logged enough hours with him to write him a real good introduction."

It is my considered opinion that for a book to be successful the author must be familiar with his subject and even better, a part of it. That the author of this book is—whatever else may be wanting. It has been claimed, for instance, that hillbillies go barefoot and I can remember when the author used to go about as barefoot as an unshod colt. Likewise, it is commonly thought that the hillbilly is ignorant; and if so, I can commend this book to you, for in this trait the author ranks in the forefront of his compatriots. In recent times the hillbilly has been widely depicted as stricken with abject poverty and to this experience the author need not take a back seat to any pauper. In fact, I have often considered requesting that his congressman submit a bill to devote an entire poverty project to relieve his acute want. I think these credentials are sufficient to establish this writer's authority on hillbilly life. In my opinion this book gives a delightful vignette of hillbilly life a couple of generations back, its humor, its institutions, its customs and language—all written in the inimitable style of my favorite author.

I think you might enjoy this book, but in case you don't, it will furnish you opportunity to palm off some bad reading on someone whom for lack of better instruments you would like to bore to death. If perchance you like this lore, commend the book to a friend in order that this struggling writer might no longer have to dig roots and herbs to earn his keep.

ONE

THE WEST VIRGINIA THAT WAS

The aim of this initial chapter is to depict the West Virginia that was about 60 years before it was discovered by the Kennedys and *The Saturday Evening Post*—when she was still a virgin.

A state too far south to be Yankee, too far north to be Dixie, and too proud to care less, West Virginia has always been just high enough to feel a little bit above her lowland neighbors.

Our pride never has been deterred by jibes of those who shrugged us off as "hillbillies," which in fact we were. We have always felt a little nearer heaven than the lowland states, heirs of the land of promise flowing with milk and and honey, not to mention an endless supply of refreshing "mountain dew." Besides the air was purer, the sparkling water cleaner, the sky bluer, the moon bigger, the sun brighter, the fishing better, and the people friendlier than any lowland spot on earth. The highest compliment ever paid a foreign state was when somebody dubbed West Virginia "the little Switzerland of America."

I can remember when West Virginia was a land of magnificent virgin forests abounding with every variety of the mighty oak, the stately poplar, and the towering pine. And let us not forget the hemlock, the greatest of the evergreens and unknown in much of the country. There was also the chestnut and what memories it recalls! Never on this earth did there flourish a tree like the native chestnut. At one time it grew in such abundance in West Virginia that a small child could pick a bushel of nuts in a single hour. It furnished bountiful food for game as well as man. Chestnut-fed hogs were as fat and had meat as sweet as cornfed swine. But this great tree has passed away and it demise marks the end of an era as well as the beginning of a tragedy. Other trees which graced these majestic virgin woodlands were the hickory and the lynn and all other trees native to this part of North America. It is an unhappy thought that such forests will never again be seen.

The natural opulence of early West Virginia was more than skin-deep, however. In the bosom of its mountain terrain, the state cradled some of the richest deposits of bituminous coal in the entire country, together with an abundance of oil and gas and great beds of salt and salt brine.

For the modern sportsman the West Virginia that was would have been paradise, a real-life happy hunting ground. The woods were literally creeping with squirrel, grouse, and raccoon as well as a bountiful population of bear, deer, and wild turkey. The fishing was enough to pop the angler's eye right out of his head. Every little mountain stream as wide as six feet and as deep as eight inches had native brook trout. Other game fish fertilely inhabited the rivers, but the brook trout was the king of the mountain fish and West Virginia was his home state.

The people who inhabit these hills have been traditionally a friendly, neighborly people. Whatever his liabilities in other states, the hillbilly has never lagged in neighborly virtue.

Until modern times the hillbilly could number among his virtues a healthy spirit of self-sufficiency. As we used to say, "every kettle must stand on its own bottom," and it was a matter of pride to do this as far as possible. It was the custom to offer or receive help only when it was genuinely needed. When the need was legitimate, help was never lacking or long in coming. It was common law that one must go to the aid of a neighbor in distress. Often when a man was ill, his neighbors milked his cows, tended his livestock, cultivated his crops, and threshed his grain.

In the old days cash was almost as scarce as June snow. However, if one had good crops and plenty of stock, little money was needed, for most transactions back then were by the barter method. If a neighbor had an extra ham, one might trade him an extra stack of hay. Or someone might trade a horse for a milkcow. It was a matter of honor to out-trade your neighbor and much practice honed one's skill. Even the community store was the scene of much over-the-counter dickering. The merchant expected it and played along. The customer tried to "due down" the merchant who was usually astute enough to allow him to succeed. The storekeeper rarely lost anything because the shrewder ones anticipated this haggling and had prices their goods accordingly. Nevertheless, it was a little ritual the hillbilly insisted on.

What cash we had in those times was generally secured from the sale of wool, sheep, or cattle. Some farmers raised potatoes and got cash for them. With just twenty-five dollars one could purchase a small wagon load of groceries, including a barrel of flour and a hundred pounds of sugar. Money, although it was

6

harder to come by then, obviously went further than it does nowadays.

Almost everyone kept chickens and surplus eggs were traded at the store for additional groceries. Most people back then canned and cured their own meat and everybody canned wild strawberries, blackberries, and even elderberries.

I think any oldtimer will agree that no modern frozen meat will compare with the cold-packed beef and pork of yesterday. It was simply scrumptious and in mountain idiom, that means several times better than delicious.

Another of the traits that used to distinguish inhabitants of these West Virginia hills was their resourcefulness. This enabled them to adhere to the independence their pride insisted on. Each man not only provided his own food by farming, trading, and hunting, but also served as his own blacksmith, carpenter, shoemaker, and perhaps even gunsmith. His wife spun, weaved, and carded the material for their clothing and made soap for the family.

Each community generally had its own gristmill and there the hillbilly ground his own wheat, corn, and buckwheat. In addition, he canned sausage and learned to grind cane for cane molasses. In the early spring when the sap was beginning to rise in the sugar trees, they tapped the trees by boring small holes in them and inserting "spiles," which were handmade spouts which allowed the sap to run from the tree into a vessel or trough of some sort. From there it was transferred to a great kettle and boiled down to maple sugar or syrup. The combination of sausage, buckwheat cakes, and maple syrup made an incomparable breakfast.

Resourceful as he was, the hillbilly had to work hard. For example, much of the grain he raised had to be threshed by hand even as late as the 1920's until threshing machines were more widely available. Hand threshing required the use of an instrument known as a "flail," a primitive threshing tool dating back almost 3,000 years. Just like the Volkswagen, the model never changed. Any museum without a flail is lacking in historical substance. When he had threshed his grain, the hillbilly farmer often cleaned it by means of a "windmill," a hand-cranked contraption no longer used. It was an ingenious invention for removing the chaff and impurities from grain and I understand the Smithsonian Institute now has one on exhibit.

I had often wondered whether it might have curbed modern juvenile delinquency if these shaggy-haired creeps who loaf

7

about town these days moaning about "nothing to do," who drive expensive cars six blocks to school, had been raised with a flail in one hand and a windmill crank in the other. Even yet they might be redeemed if we could resurrect the cranky one-room schoolteacher who would flail them. It was actually discovered in those days what seems to have been forgotten since, that the judicious application of a hickory switch was a tremendous leavening influence on youth.

Today's beer drinking fathers and bowling mothers and television children know nothing of the wholesome family atmosphere and community life of that day. People did not live easy lives, but they did live useful ones. Everyone assumed the responsibility of making his contribution. They learned to share their blessings and they learned to share their sorrows. That way of life seems now to be gone forever.

West Virginia was settled almost exclusively by Anglo Saxons. The westward drift across the mountains to what is now West Virginia began around 1750. The early settlers were not shiftless men, but rather men of character and purpose who were willing to pay the price for a life of their own unfettered by regulations of Mother England and the colonial establishment of eastern Virginia. They resented what they considered taxation without representation. So they faced the peril of the savage, the dangers of unknown mountains and uncharted forests for that precious privilege of freedom. These settlers brought with them their ways and their language, a culture short on refinement, but rich in color, simplicity, and individualism. This culture with its language, customs, and music remained intact better than that of any other region, a fact attributable perhaps in part to the isolation of the mountaineer. But the major factor is the rugged individualism of the hillbilly. The true mountaineer is no conformist or he would have stayed east of the Alleghenies.

The typical hillbilly was a God-fearing man imbued with the teachings of the Old Testament. He was as a rule puritanically moral and believed implicitly in hellfire and damnation. Hillbillies were stern parents who believed in a stern God and as one would expect, they raised their children in strict discipline. When the parent spoke, the children jumped—in nothing flat. As they themselves often expressed it, they raised their younguns "by the hair of their heads." For all his severity, the hillbilly parent was equally just in dealing with his children. He just happened to subscribe to that principle in

8

urgent need of revival today: "spare the rod and spoil the child."

It must be admitted that a hillbilly is a peculiar creature like the mountain sheep and inhabitants of high places the earth over. He is different from those ordinary mortals who populate the lowlands and the crowded cities and other people whose horizon is limited by their environment. His hillbilly ways have been the object of much fun-making by some and his peculiarities are generally conceded by outsiders to be a strike against his good sense. Whatever his popular image, the fact is that West Virginians never have been beggers for native intelligence except in things political. In political affairs, it must be conceded that the ignorance of West Virginians is second only to a retarded jackass. But nobody is equally smart across the board and scores of hillbillies have distinguished themselves in the business and academic world.

There was a time in fact when it took a little ingenuity and imagination to survive in these hills, for it is only in recent years that the government has stepped in with its dole and bureaucratic approach to Appalachian problems and relieved us of the responsibility of "hoeing our own row," as every hillbilly was once expected and even proud to do.

It was our forebears of whom George Washington spoke in the darkest hours of the Revolution when as a last resort he talked of planting his banners in the hills of West Agusta, for the hillbilly was a fierce fighting man with a will to battle to the bitter end. He did honestly feel that he could fight better, run faster, jump higher and spit farther than any lowlander alive.

History will confirm that out of these hills have proceeded some outstanding military leaders of whom General "Stonewall" Jackson was one, some distinguished medical men, some well-known newsmen, and not a few commercial leaders. What history will overlook is that fact that these hills have also spawned some of the most proficient, extraordinary moonshiners this earth has ever seen. These men could take a cornfield and convert it into the highest proof courtin' and fightin' liquor that has ever graced this earth. No ordinary moonshiners, these men could turn an orchard into apple brandy worthy of a king. One moonshiner in our area used to ask the customer whether he wanted courtin' or fightin' liquor. He guaranteed his fightin' liquor to make a man a match for John L. Sullivan and his courtin' liquor to transform a customer into a lover greater than Romeo. Not being a drinking man, I cannot vouch

9

for his claims; but he did a land office business with no refunds.

Most of the community life in those days centered around the churches and schools, especially the churches. There the young were taken for christening and the dead for burial. It was there that boy met girl and I can testify from experience that this factor alone made avid churchgoers of the younger generation. Fortunately, a little rubbed off on some which undoubtedly helped the moral climate in those days.

This is a rough sketch of the West Virginia that was. I would'nt want to retreat into the past, but I expect many of my readers would share the hope that one day we might retrieve the best of the past to replace the worst of the present.

TWO

MOUNTAIN LANGUAGE

West Virginia, perhaps better than any other area of this country, has preserved the mid-Victorian language of her infancy. While the mountainous areas of North Carolina and Tennessee have much in common with our state in this respect, the West Virginia dialect has not been crossed with its southern counterpart.

As someone once described the accent of Jerry West, a native West Virginian whose name became familiar to sport fans of all America as the superstar of the Los Angeles Laker basketball team, the West Virginia dialect is "three parts sweet potato, one part magnolia, two parts coonskin, and a sprinkling of Elizabethan moonshine English."

Back in the hills the language remains very much as it was 100 years ago. It is a colorful vernacular, expressive and exciting and right to the point. It is charming and completely authentic, unlike the artificial styles of modern bohemians and beatniks who strain themselves to be different. But our mountain idiom is reminescent of the language of Shakespeare with a hillbilly twang.

Since time is slowly but gradually eroding the use of mountain expressions, I would like to salvage for posterity some familiarity with it. In addition to a brief, but representative glossary of colorful mountain idioms, I want to share with the reader a letter from an old mountain friend, Professor J.H. Groves, now of Georgia, written at my request. In this masterful letter, Prof. Groves helpfully reverts to hillbilly vernacular, illustrating for the uninitiated reader the usage of scores of favorite mountain expressions. The letter is as follows, with many of the more outstanding mountainisms italicized:

Dear Granville,

With pen in hand I will write you a few lines to let you know I am well and hope you are the same.

When I get to thinking and talking about those old words and phrases that we used way back yonder some

11

sixty years ago, *pears* like I kinda forget to talk good grammar and slip back into the vernacular that we used in the Bend of Deer Crick, Kentucky *Deestrict*, Nicholas County, West Virginia.

Even though I have a pretty good start down the *Western Slope*, and although my head is *blooming for the grave*, and while the *Vicissitudes of time* have wrought some havoc on my being, yet, I can recall many things that happened when I was just a *chunk of a boy*, how the people talked, the expressions they used, the strange way they did their work, and so many words which we used that have become almost extinct in this modern age, which at that time was our common everyday language. Were it possible for a group of the Old people who lived in that age to get together again and speak in that tongue, the present generation would think that we were a *Parcel of furriners*. In writing this letter to you I shall lapse quite a bit into that Old Tongue.

I want to say right now that *jist* as soon as I complete this *missive*, I am going to *Back* it (address it) and take it to the post office and mail it, for if I don't, I'll forgit if I let it lay around. My Uncle John Will Groves used to say *Procrastination Is a Thief of time*. Our post office aint too fur away and is right *ferninth* the court house.

I went to the *Bend* School out in the *Corner*. We like to get to school quite a while before the *Books Took Up* so we could play Shoot The Buck, Anty Over, Prisoner's Base, Fox and Goose, or Townball. When *Books Let Out* we had to hurry home as fast as *Shanks Filly* would take us to *Do Up The Turns*.

We did our *ciphering* on slates and saved our *slick tablet paper* to write our *compositions* on. Some of the more *Well-to-do Scholars* wrote their compositions on *Fools Cap Paper*. I could *parse* words and diagram sentences real good but talked awful poor *grammar*. The *scholars* made fun of anybody that *Talked proper*.

It always made me have a very happy *feelin* in my *innards* when we had a *last day* at our school. I just loved to hear the scholars say their *pieces* and speak their *declamations*. We had *Spelling Matches* the Last Day and although I was poor in *orthography* and got *turned down* a lot, yet, I liked to take part. I think that I

12

got the prize for getting the most *Head-Marks* just one year when I went to school and that was the year that Jinny Dooley was *Poorly* and missed a lot of school with the *tisic* (pthisic).

My ma was a mighty good woman. She could throw a *Meals Vittles* together as *quick as a cat could wink its eye*, and what I want to tell you is, that when you *munched some of ma's cookin*, you really and truly *relished your grub*. I have gone to the table with my stomach feeling a bit *dauncy* and felt that I couldn't eat anything, but after I had taken a bite of her *sweetened pone*, nibbled on a *shank dumplin*, or took a mouthful of *souse fried in batter*, then I started eatin with a *coming appetite*, and before you knowed it, I was eating like a hungry *grubber*. My, my, but I did like her *pie-plant* pies (rhubarb), and there was no one that could *cook up a mess* of *handovers* (rutabagas) better than ma.

She was a mighty handy in *working up wool*. After we had *clipped* the sheep and plucked the wool, pa would take it to the *Carding Machine* and get it turned into *rolls* and then ma would *set in* to spinning. She was the best spinner that lived *over on our side* of Gauley River. She could spin 12 *cuts* a day and be through by *half-after-three*. Three cuts make a *Hank* and I'll tell you this right now, anybody who can spin more than four hanks a day *hast to git up before breakfast*. I used to *piddle around* and git in ma's way while she was spinning and she would give me a crack over the *noggin* with the *spinning stick*. When the *spindle* on her wheel got full of yarn, she would wound it off on the *Reel*. There was a little strip of hickory wood on the reel that would crack when she wound off a *cut*. The cut was taken off the reel and put on the *Winding Blades*, and from this I had to wind the cut into a ball of yarn. Ma used this ball of yarn to knit and I'm a tellin you, she did a lot of *knittin*. She knit our socks, mittens, the girl's *half-handers* and sometimes she would knit their *fascinators*. The girls liked *store-boughten* fascinators better though, because the ones that they got at the store had more Gew-Gaw's on them. Ma did a lot of weaving, too, and it *vexed* and *aggravated* her a *heap* cause pa wouldn't make her a pair of *Warping Bars*. Every time that she had to get the *warp* for a *weavin*

13

she had to go over to Aunt Cindy's to use her Warping Bars.

My pa was a mighty good man, too. He was a *God-Fearen*, honest, sober, *awful clever*, and very *Work-Brittle*. He was very *handy* and could do *pretty neart* anything *he had a mind* to do. He could *tack* a shoe on a horse, *rive* shingles with a *fro*, hew sills with a *broad-axe* and shave shingles on a *shingle-horse*. He could doctor a horse with the *botts*, a cow with the *foot-evil*, a sheep with the *rickets*, and a hog with the *quinsy*.

He was a mighty good judge of Split-Timber. I never knew him to cut a *split-stick* out of a white-oak *saplin*, but what it made *fur-strait splits*. Everybody said that pa was a *Right Hand* when it come to splitting rails. He could get more rails out of the timber than most men. I have known him to get twenty rails out of one *rail cut*. Of course, this would be the *butt cut*. While splitting rails he would never use a *nigger-maul*. He used a *knot-maul*, one *Ironwedge* and three or four *sour-wood gluts*. He always *snaked* his rail timber with a single horse and a *bull-hook*. Not that pa couldn't drive a team *hooked in double*—he was good with the check-lines— but one horse could get through the underbrush better. He was one of the first men in our neighborhood to build *stake-and-rider* instead of the old time *Worm Fence*.

I could never throw the *gears* on the horses to suit pa. He would always find something wrong. The *hame-string* would be twisted, the *belly band* would not be tight enough, always complained the way I had the *breechin* hooked up, and would tighten the *crupper strap* up another hole. He always changed the shoulder pads to they would not rub the horses *withers*.

Pa was a pretty good hand with the Mountain Rifle. We just loved to see him throw a bar of lead in the *melting Ladle*, and it *peard* like that before you could say *Jack Robinson*, that lead would be *het up* to the *molten* stage so pa could pour it in the *bullet molds* and make bullets. When he loaded the gun, he would press a bullet down in the muzzle of the *barl* and trim the *patchin* off with his *I.X.L. knife*, then he would push the bullet clear down to the *breech* with his *ram-rod*. Of

14

course, he always poured a *charge* of powder in the barl before he puts the bullet in. Sometimes the powder would be a bit damp and the old rifle would make a *long fire*. He always carried his accessories in the *Shot pouch*. Our shotgun was a *breech loader*, but the mountain rifle was a *muzzle-loader*. We fired the shotgun *off-hand*, but always took a rest when we aimed the rifle.

When pa *vexed* or *aggravated* or *tormented* ma about something, she would throw up to him that he was *penurious* about his *eatin*. He claimed that Sweetened Pone gave him the *dyspepsia* and that *polk greens* and fodder beans wasn't fit for a dog to eat. You couldn't get him to even touch anything that had been *put up in air-tight jars*.

Pa helped *clear* and *red up* a lot of ground. He was mighty good with a *hacking-axe*, a *pole-axe*, or a *double-bitted axe*. He wasn't as *stout* (strong) as Cousin Homer Britt, but he was mighty *withey* and could bring his end of a *Hand-Spike* up with men a whole lot bigger than him. The general opinion was that pa could *pack* (carry) a powerful heavy load for a man of his size.

In the Meeting House he was not considered *able* in prayer and never *took too much* to giving long experiences in *Speakin Meetin*, but in *Preachin Meetin*, *Class Meetin*, and *Protracted Meetins* he led the singing for years. He knew both the *shape notes* and the *round notes* and was able to get the right pitch of a *tune* without a *tuning-fork*. Cousin Edbert was very able in prayer and my cousin Joel Hill could talk better in Speakin Meetin than a lot of *licensed exhorters*.

Pa didn't whittle as much as a lot of fellers. He *marked* a lot of stock and he always wanted a keen edge on his blade. I well remember our mark. It was a *crop* and a *split* out of the right ear and an *underbit* out of the left ear. Uncle Mansfield's mark was a crop and a split out of the left ear and a *top bit* out of the right ear. These marks were used only on sheep and hogs, and especially hogs. If a person found a sheep or hog out in the woods unmarked, they could claim the animal as their own. Sometimes a sow would have a litter of pigs out in the woods and *un-be-knownst* to the owner of the sow and they would not be marked. The sires of these pigs would usually have poor *stock* in them and would be known as *ridge-runners* or *sand-splitters*. After these pigs grew into *shoats*, and the shoats grew into *killin-hogs*, there was usually a pretty good *mast* and these unmarked hogs would get fat and it was great sport to hunt them. These unmarked pigs were known as *Mast-Pigs* and this was the origin of illegitimate children being called mast-pigs as well as *wood-colts*.

Going to the store was quite a chore for lads of *them days*. Oft times I have gone to the store with three or four old hens that were not paying for their *keep* as egg producers, a few dozen eggs, and a couple pounds of butter. I would get only a few items of immediate need and get the rest in a *due-bill*. Later ma would go to the store and *lift the due-bill*. The items which I purchased would usually be a *nut-meg*, a can of *lamp-oil*, a spool of *Number 8 white O.N.T. thread*, and a box of *clinching tacks*. Once in a great while he would let me get a five-cent *poke* of peppermint stick candy.

Courting was a lot different in Them Days from what it is now. The real sport would be clad in *full-peg britchers*, a shiny high stiff collar, a *tolable* flashy *cravat*, and if he was in his *shirt-sleeves*, fancy *sleeve-holders* and showy *galluses* helped a lot to adorn his *raiment*. "May I See You Home," or "May I Carry Your Umbrella," was the first approach that a young squire made on his fair lady, and if she refused his request, it was known far and wide that the young man had been *sacked*. If she said "yes," and they got along well, then they started *keeping company*. If they lived in different neighborhoods, they exchanged *Billy-Doos* (love letters). When the young feller got to liking the girl better than he liked himself, he would *Pop the Question*, and if she liked him the same way, she would say "yes," and pretty soon they would *jump the broom stick*. The wedding took place at the home of the bride, but the *infair* was held at the groom's *place of abode*.

We always drove our cows up to the *milk-gap* before we *pailed* them. If the cow was *Fresh* we let her *suckle* her calf and then we *stripped* her. Ma was mighty particular about us getting all the *strippins*. She said that a pint of strippins was worth as much as a

16

half-gallon of *fore-milk* for making up a *churnin*. My, O my, but I hated to churn! I was a whole lot like what the *feller said* about churnin. He said that he would *druther* be dead than cut corn, but still he'd *sooner* cut corn than churn. After I had brought that old *churn-dasher* up and down two hundred times and the butter didn't start to come, then I would squall for the hot water. Ma was awful slow though about bringing out the *tea-kittle*, for if there was anything that she *abominated* that was *scalded butter*. If you did not *drive* a cow when she got to *Cuttin-Up* and let her *git with calf*, then she would run a stripper for a year, then they usually *beefed* her. When you were going to *beef a cow*, you usually fed her a lot of *fodder* and *nubbins*.

Our pa was awful strict with us *younguns*. When he told us to do something, we did it right now, for we knew that what pa said was *the word with the bark on it*. He never *whuped* us much, but when he did *tan our hides*, we knowed that we had been *thrashed*. Ma *withed* us quite a bit, but we never *paid much mind* to her *sproutings*. Pa always argued that a little *Hickory-tea* was good to make a youngun grow.

In my young days there was a lot of *rassling* done. They just stepped right up and took *fair and square* back holts and then went to it *hip and thigh, tooth and toenail* and *fist and skull*. If they hit the ground *along side of each other*, it was a *dog-fall*, but if one feller was on top of the other feller, then he had *"Dirtied His Back."*

I would *venture the assertation* that I had lived through some thirteen or fourteen *chestnut harvests* before I ever saw a doctor in our house. A *granny-woman* delivered all of our children and for most of our ailments we had home remedies. *Catnip, tansy,* and *peppermint* teas were given to babies, and for bad colds we took *Penteroil* (pennyroyal) and *Boneset* teas. Sulphur and molasses were taken in the spring to clean up our blood and we wore *sulphur pokes* around our necks to keep from gittin the *seven-year-each*. If we took the *each* in spite of this precaution, then we greased our bodies with *sulphur and Fat*. For minor ailments we took a dose of oil and turpentine, but if we became *just real poorly*, we took a *through of*

17

calomel. Sheep-manure tea was good for *bringing out the measles*, and *bermafuge* was our number one worm medicine. Some of our most popular patent medicines or tonics were "Bliss Native Herbs," "Dr. Pierce's Golden Medical Discovery," "Perunia The Great Tonic," "Honey Tolou," "Barkers Nerve Bone and Linament," and "Lydia E. Pinkhams Vegetable Compound." The only patent medicine that has remained with me from infancy up to the present day is "Chas. Fletcher's Castoria."

Superstition played a major role in the lives of the natives in them good old days. Seeds were planted when the *signs were right*. If cabbage plants were set out in the *sign of the root*, it never *headed* to do any good and potatoes planted in the *sign of the head* went to tops and the *taters* just wouldn't *tater*. The ends of *clap-boards* would curl if they were put on a building in the light of the moon. If you killed hogs when the moon was not right, then the meat would *render* very little lard. It was a dire tragedy for a bird to fly into your bedroom or to dream of fresh meat, for those were sure signs of death. If you nose itched, someone was sure to come visiting and if you dropped your *dishrag* on the floor, then the visitor would be of bad repute. We dared not raise an umbrella in a room, walk under a ladder, or continue our journey after a black cat had crossed our path. We dreaded the seven-years bad luck we would have when we broke a *looking glass*. If it rained during a funeral, it was a sure sign the departed had *gone right*, but the hearts of close friends were heavy should the *burryin* be on a pretty day.

A wart could be removed if rubbed with a piece of *mullen leaf* and the piece of leaf placed under a flat rock in the third *fence corner* away. When the mullen leaf rotted, then the wart disappeared. When we had a sty on the eye, we went to *End of the Lane,* clear out to the *Big Road* and said: "Sty, Sty, Go Off My Eye And Go On To The Next Person That Passes By."

Tooth dentists were as scarce those days as *Hen's Teeth*. We had an old blacksmith in our community that had a pair of *Tooth-Drawers* that would yank one out if your toothache gave you too much misery.

Folks who were lacking and had no *Git-Up* about

18

them were considered *Kinda Doolis,* and the general idea was that they would never *set the world on fire.* They were not worth the *salt in their bread* and hardly worth the *powder and lead it would take to blow them up.*

When folks became such good friends that they started *peain through the same quill,* were together all the time and what one did, so did the *tother,* then the general comment was that they were getting *too thick.* And *Mind Right Now What I'm Tellin You,* They Are Going To Have *A Fallin-Out* and the next thing you know, they won't be *Speaken.* We *calculated* that it *weren't a good idy* to *git as thick as Cherry and Brindle, Three in a bed* or as *Thick as Peas In A Pod.* Sometimes when they had a fallin-out, they would be mad at each other and wouldn't make up till the next Protracted Meetin.

Our solemn oaths to secrecy were "Cross My Heart I Hope To Die," "Drop Dead," or "Goodman Knows It," and when this oath was given, we knew that the secret we told was locked in the breast of the listener.

Common expressions were: "Quick as a Fairy-diddle," "Slick as a Whistle," "Fast as Greased Lightning," "Slow as Cold Molasses," "Dumb as an Ox," "Rough as a Rasp," "Pretty as a Speckled Pup," "Ugly as a Mud Fence Lined with Tad-poles," "Smart as a Whip," "Sharp as a Tack," "Happy as a Coon in the Cornfield," "Blind as a Bat," "Cold as an Iron Wedge," and "Hot as Blue Blazes."

When folks thought *more seemly* of themselves than they should, they were classed as being "Stuck-up" or having the "Big-Head."

When *topors* partook too much of the wine when it was *red in the cup,* they became "Full as a Tick," "Higher than a Kite," "Tighter than a Boot," "Higher than a Georgia Pine," "So High They Couldn't Hit the Ground with Their Hat," "Liquored to the Gills," "Three Sheets in the Wind," and drunk as a "Fiddler's Bitch."

Certain individuals when asked if they know someone, their reply would be: "I Wouldn't Know Them If I Met Them in the Big Road," "I Wouldn't Know Him from a Side of Sole-Leather," or "I

Wouldn't Know Him from Adam's Off-Ox."

The good church member would not use profanity at all, but they had some pretty good substitutes when they felt that they just had to *give vent to their spleen.* Once I heard Uncle Oss Bryant hurl *scathing denunciations* and *vile invectives* at his team when his *off-horse* Frank was *acting real ornery and contrary* during *fly-time* while he was plowing for late buckwheat. His *vituperations* sounded as follows while he berated his *infernlous aggravatin beasts:* "Git up, there, Frank, you *Dad-Blasted, Dad-Burned, Dad-Shamed Triflin* Old Devil. I Do Hope That the Good Lord God Almighty Strikes You Dead with the Botts before the Settin Sun, So Help Me God, I Do."

Soap Makin was a pretty big April chore at our house. During the winter Ma would save all her hickory ashes for her lye. *Bout* the first of March she would start fussin at Pa to build the *Ash-hopper.* After this important edifice had been erected, then she would run off her lye. At Hog-Killen time she *red the guts* to get the *soap grease.* Then the lye was put in with the soap grease and this mixture was dumped into a large iron *kittle* and after it was *biled* for about three days, we had our home-made soap for the next year. *Nature in the Raw is seldom mild* and I found this out when I used it to *set my reach.* After applying a good application of the stuff on a roach and go out in the cold weather, the hair in my roach would get as stiff as *hog bristles.* When I entered the school room and stood before the red-hot stove for awhile, the soap would start to thaw and the lye would drool down in my eyes and made them smart to beat *blixen.*

Going to *Night Meetin* was a mighty big event in my young days. The first few days of a protracted Meetin was taken up with the regular church members getting the *harness on* and getting *warmed up* to do good personal work on the *sinners* and *backsliders.* During this warm-up period there were no evening services. After the church members got the harness well adjusted and were full of the Spirit, then the preacher would announce from the pulpit: *"If There Be No Preventin Providence,* we will have meeting tonight and the service will begin at *early-lamplight."* Before

20

sinners could have any success at the *Mourner's Bench*, they had to be *under conviction* and then they would have no trouble *Prayin Through*.

When individuals suggested that they were enjoying a *reasonable portion of health and strength*, they meant that they were *tolerable stout* or *Bout as Common*. If they were *off their feed* a bit, that indicated that they were *under the weather, kinda puny*, or were *Poorly like*.

A very important structure in the church lot was the *Horse-Block, Riding-Block, Upping-Block*, or *Stile*, as it was called in different localities. The males tried to get to church quite a while before *Meetin took up* and used this structure as a social center. Here they discussed politics, religion, and crops. When a woman rode up on her *beast* sitting on a *side saddle*, the men got up from the horse-block while she made a landing. She always took off her long black riding skirt and fastened it on the side saddle before some of the men took her beast and tied it up to a nearby *hitching-post*.

Well, Granville, *Jist Pears Like* when I git to talkin about them good Old Days when we didn't keer too much about what kind of grammar we talked, that my old tongue gits *loose at both ends* and I jist don't know when to quit *runnin off at the mouth*, but I spect I had better bring this missive to a conclusion. As we review these old words, expressions, customs and habits, I have jist about come to the conclusion that TIMES AIN'T LIKE THEY USED TO BE. I KINDA FIGURE THEY ARE MORE LIKE THEY ARE NOW.

I hope that you might draw something from these jumblings that will help you in your effort.

Yours truly,

J.H. Graves
Box 64
Jefferson, Georgia

Not everyone is happy that mountain language is gradually being traded in for "proper talk." A couple of years ago a talented mountaineer by the name of Jerry Coakley protested this unseemly trend in a clever poem published in the *Webster*

Republican. His spirited defense of hill talk appeared as follows:

Now we don't mind if folks declare
That mountaineers are dumb and square
Or make a fuss cause we're not neat
Have knobby knees and paddle feet.
But it riles a man and makes us wonder
When folks make fun of saying "Yonder."
Because they swear and us folks "cuss,"
And cause they quarrel while we folks "fuss."
Now when we go to milk they wail,
"That there's a bucket, not a 'pail'!"
They shake their heads and have the cheek,
To laugh at "crick" instead of creek.
A "get together's" got to be,
A meeting like for you and me.
When they get hurt they never "squal"
They sigh and cry, not even "bawl."
A "heart attack" now mercy me,
Thrombosis is the word you see.
Say "tote" or pack they're sure to grin,
And "poke" for a bag is most a sin.
What's a "tater" friend? they'll say
"Are roast'nears edible, tell us pray."
No "honky-tonk" will get their trade,
A tavern's much, much higher grade.
A hot cake they will not agree
Is just a "flitter" or can't see
How we can even wed a wife
Our style of courtin' got no life.
There's lots more things that I could tell,
[Don't dast repeat that old word "Yell."]
I'm certain sure to end this story.

A BRIEF GLOSSARY OF TYPICAL
MOUNTAIN WORDS AND EXPRESSIONS

WORD OR EXPRESSION	DEFINITION
1. *ferninth*	across from or opposite
2. *antigodlin* [or *sigodlin*]	out of plumb
3. *fetch*	to bring

4. *rench* . . . . to rinse
5. *hanker* . . . . to desire
6. *ketched* . . . . caught
7. *buss* . . . . kiss
8. *heft* [*or hefty*] . . . . large or strong
9. *tote* . . . . to carry
10. *tisic* . . . . an imaginary ailment
11. *dauncy* . . . . particular about food or dress
12. *swarp* . . . . to strike or hit
13. *hassle* . . . . to fight
14. *tater* . . . . potato
15. *bumfuzzled* . . . . confused
16. *smothersome* . . . . lacking air or oxygen
17. *skunned* . . . . skinned
18. *afeared* . . . . to be afraid
19. *han't* . . . . ghost
20. *t'aint so* . . . . not true
21. *Hell's smidgin* . . . . a large number or quantity
22. *a rasslin fool* . . . . a good wrestler
23. *p'int blank* . . . . the image of
24. *show actor* . . . . an actor
25. *store-clothes* . . . . store-bought apparel
26. *biscuit-bread* . . . . a biscuit
27. *light-bread* . . . . bread baked in loaf form
28. *loud-cusser* . . . . one given to loud profanity
29. *fish-kechinest* . . . . an expert fisherman
30. *calf-meat* . . . . veal
31. *triflin cuss* . . . . lazy workman
32. *kinda puny* . . . . prone to be ill
33. *weed-monkey* . . . . an immoral woman
34. *He'd chase a flea across Africa for the tallow* . . . . . .
. . . . stingy or miserly
35. *He's a self-made S.O.B.* . . . .
. . . . A S.O.B. with no reflection of parentage
36. *He'd charge Hell with only a water bucket* . . . .
. . . . unusually courageous or nervy
38. *Going down the Western Slope* . . . . getting old
39. *Blooming for the grave* . . . . hair turning gray
40. *He don't have the brains God gave a goose* . . . .
. one characterized by ignorance or poor judgment
41. *One could han't a house with her face* . . . .
. . . . a woman so ugly she could haunt a house
42. *I had a feelin' in my bones* . . . .

...................foreboding of something
43. *ornery* ....a catch-all word for most of the bad
in the human race
44. *He's a twenty-two jewled tomcat* ....a devil
with the women
45. *He's a slick talker alright* .....someone too smooth
to be sincere
46. *He can lie faster than a horse can run* ....
.........................a pathological liar
47. *His own hogs won't cum when he calls 'em* ....
...........................the same as above
48. *He kicked the bucket* ....died
49. *They fit fist and skull* ....fought with no regard
for rules or ethics
50. *She fell hard enuf to break her looking glass* ......
...........a woman falling hard on the south end
51. *Hoe your own row* ....be self-sufficient
52. *Every kettle should stand on its own bottom* ......
...........................same as above

SOME MOUNTAIN DESCRIPTIVE PHRASES

1. *It's colder than a witch's heart.*
2. *The man's so contrary, if you throw him in the river he'd float upstream.*
3. *Naked as a jaybird.*
4. *Her tongue wags at both ends.*
5. *Her tongue is a mile long.*
6. *It's blue cold.*
7. *The boy's so cross-eyed, he could stand in the middle of the week and see both Sundays.*
8. *No, the baby didn't come early; the wedding came late.*
9. *It's hotter than the hinges of hell.*
10. *I was so dizzy I had to hold onto the grass afore I could lean against the ground.*
11. *I sez, sez I, to myself...*
12. *I done sent do it.*
13. *Naked as a hound dog's rump.*

THREE

THE ONE-ROOM SCHOOLHOUSE

One of the most remarkable institutions of mountain culture at the turn of the century was the one-room schoolhouse. Although a few such schools still remain in the more remote areas of some counties, the one-room school is virtually extinct, so much so that most mountain youngsters today have never seen one.

In its heyday, however, it was the ultimate academic institution for the average mountaineer. And as a social center of the community, it was second only to the church. There were held those memorable "box suppers" where mischievous young swains would often conspire to embarrass a friend by teaming up their money, forcing him to bid higher than he could afford for the privilege of sitting with his favorite girl.

Education in the one-room schools lacked the breadth and sophistication of our modern institutions. Basically, it was a simple "bread and butter" education concentrating almost exclusively on the Three-R's—'readin,' 'ritin,' and 'rithmetic. If the one-room schoolteacher was a jack of few trades, it must be said to his everlasting credit, he generally got across what his modern counterpart under vastly more ideal conditions seems unable to teach. The educational values of the one-room school were such that to be "spelled down" was well-nigh a disgrace and woe betide the student who failed to master McGuffey's Reader or Ray's Arithmetic.

High schools in those days were literally few and far between. Consequently, many students continued to attend these one-room schools until they were 17 or so. As the boys were fully grown by this time and the girls attractively matured, the one-room school was a garden of romance in which many a mountain marriage blossomed.

The Bible promises that "the meek shall inherit the earth." However, with all due respect to the meek, they did not last long enough in the one-room school to inherit anything. In most country schools there were some young behemoths muscular enough to whip a bear with a switch and they were pretty hard on the meek. Ordinarily though, the one-room teacher was a worthy adversary. One such teacher was called in to quell an insurrection at a chronically embattled school. He was a convinced adherent of the "switch-first-ask-questions-later" school. The first day on the job he rang the bell with unaccustomed authority and ordered the young rebels to be seated. After a quick survey of the enemy, he fingered the biggest, most belligerent-looking student in the class:

"Hey, you! Come up here!"

Not easily bluffed, the hulking boy sauntered indifferently toward the front of the room as the teacher reached for an inconspicuous hickory switch. Then, like an angry rattler, except without warning, the teacher uncoiled on his unsuspecting victim, striking him with almost dangerous enthusiasm.

As he finished, his startled, but refreshingly subdued 'example' yelped woundedly:

"Whut did ya do that fur? I han't done nuthin!"

"For looking so damned impudent," responded the new teacher, exuding a profound lack of remorse that did not escape the notice of the astonished class.

After that show of raw force, the school was persuaded that indiscipline was no longer a live option.

'Communication' between parents and teachers was a problem even in the one-room schoolhouse era. I have often wondered if the modern PTA was not inspired by the Sid Stull incident. A young teacher, fresh out of an eight grade post-graduate course known as "summer college," which was required for a teaching certificate, was hired to teach at the school Sid attended. One day in the course of a history lesson, she asked Sid:

"Who signed the Declaration of Independence?"

"Damned if I know," Sid shrugged. Startled, she asked him again and got the same response.

Mortified at such uncouth language from a student, the young maiden teacher resolved to take firm disciplinary action. That afternoon she sent a note by Sid to his father giving him the exact question she had asked Sid and his response and informing him that Sid was thereby suspended from classes until he could give a proper answer. The next morning at school, she found to her surprise father and son occupying the same seat. As class took up Mr. Stull rose to his feet and addressed the young teacher with gentlemanly respect:

"Miz Sears, I got your note about Sid and I want to say I

don't have no book larnin' and neither does his ma, but we are God fearin' folks and has always tried to do right and we want Sid to do the same.''

Then with serious countenance he turned and admonished Sid:

"Now Sid, if you signed that damned thing, confess to it and take your punishment.''

Our county superintendents were elected and, like the circuit riding preachers, made their rounds on horseback. The object of these itineraries to every extremity of the country was to observe the various teachers and to discuss their problems. One of our former superintendents used to tell a humorous story about one of his teachers whom the superintendent found in no mood to share his problems.

The superintendent had never met this particular teacher, as the teachers on those days were hired by the three school trustees serving each community. So he made a trip to meet and to observe this new man. When he arrived, he hitched his horse near the schoolhouse and approached the building on foot. It was a balmy spring day and the door was open, enabling him as he strode toward the school to discern an angrily loud voice punctuated occasionally by vicious snaps like the crack of a whip. Drawing up to the door, he stood outside unobserved for a moment. Inside he could hear someone shouting bitterly:

"Git your lessons!" and again that peculiar cracking sound.

Curious, he finally walked inside. The voice was that of the new schoolteacher, a tall, redheaded fellow who looked as mean as a snake in dog-days. He was wielding a hickory switch big enough to frighten Samson. Impervious to the presence of the superintendent, the teacher continued every few minutes to bellow, "Git your lessons," followed by several blistering cracks of the switch on the floor. The room was quiet as death and the students seemed to be "Gittin' their lessons," the school chief recalled.

With the teacher obviously in no mood for interruptions and the superintendent being somewhat baffled by such proceedings, he left the room and went immediately to the home of a Mr. Dorsey who boarded the teacher. He told Mr. Dorsey about what he had just observed and inquired if there was some trouble at the school or if this perhaps was the teacher's usual procedure.

What Dorsey told him seemed to justify the teacher's

approach to education. During the noon hour the day before the teacher had gone down the creek for a brief swim. While he was in the water, some of the big boys stole his clothes. Finding them missing when he went to dress, he decided to slip through the woods which extended almost to the Dorsey house and hoped from there to sneak unobserved to his room and get some clothes. He hadn't reckoned on Dorsey's very fine watchdog. When he got to the edge of the woods, he was spotted by the dog which didn't recognize him in his birthday suit. Without ceremony the overly-conscientious dog treed him. All the barking brought the women to investigate, whereupon they found the embarrassed teacher up the tree helplessly glistening in the nude. The women summoned the men to rescue the teacher, who got clothed quickly and hustled back to school in an unfriendly mood.

From those naked facts, the superintendent concluded rather than risk barking up the wrong tree, it would be wiser for him to return on another occasion.

FOUR

THE COUNTRY STORE

Just as the church and the school served as the social centers of the mountain communities, a third institution, the country store, tended to become the center of economic activity.

My own community was not typical in this regard. Our neighbors were extremely hardworking people of the pioneer stripe who viewed the country store only as a place to buy necessary commodities and run an account until they sold their wool or lambs. Believing religiously in the old adage that one "must make hay while the sun shines," they had little time for loitering around the local Wall Street.

Hominy Falls, where my uncle had a store, is a more representative example. As a lad I worked there every year in my uncle's store between school terms. Each day the local male citizenry gathered there like elder statesmen to settle the fate of the world. Whether the issue was the question of a gold or a silver standard or a high or a low tariff, each considered himself a ranking authority on the matter and clung to his convictions in the face of all contrary opinion or reason. Some still were unshakeably convinced that the earth was flat, while others were equally sure it was round. No two of them could agree on the weather signs, and there were two schools of thought on whether one ought to plant in the dark or the light of the moon.

The individualism of their opinion carried over even to the brands of tobacco they chewed. As a result, my uncle stocked for their edification and his profit what undoubtedly was one of the greatest assortments of chewing tobacco anywhere. In plug tobacco he carried everything on the market, including such favorites as Browns Mule, Apple Sun Cured, and Mello Plug. And each brand had its diehard adherents. The same could be said for twist tobacco. He even stocked locally-grown twists for the benefit of community he-man types who felt the manufactured varieties weren't strong enough. He also carried a generous supply of snuffs, including the Copenhagen brand, which was recommended for supermen only, since no normal man could stand up under its power.

The one thing these chewers had in common was the incontestable distinction of being the most accurate spitters in the world of tobacco. The standard target was the pot-bellied Burnside in the country store. Normally they would aim at a small section of the stove, perhaps a spot about two inches square, from a distance of five to eleven feet. They soon reduced spitting to a fine art. Even among that select circle of eleven-foot spitters, only a few were dependably accurate at that distance. Those who were, were the envy of all young amateurs who in turn tried to emulate these marksmen and in a few cases succeeded. The less spectacular five-foot spitters had to compensate for their lack of thrust with quantity. They kept the Burnside stove spewing and sounding deceptively like a whistling tea-kettle. One fringe benefit of this aerial bombardment was that it kept the air in the store pleasantly humid.

The country store was a general store, dealing in everything from eggs to corsets to farm equipment. In case of death, even coffins and burial garments could be purchased there.

Cash was scarce, and much of the trade at the store was done on a credit basis or through the barter system. Surplus eggs, for example, could be traded for other commodities. If the customer was short of cash and had no farm produce with which to barter, the merchant credited him until he could sell some. In this way, the country merchant acted as the early forerunner to modern financial institutions.

It was the custom with most people to bargain with the merchant of the country store. He expected it and played along. If he was an astute individual, he generally allowed himself to be "dued down" a little. It was a subtle public relations gesture, as each patron took great pride in "duing down" the price of the merchandise. Of course, the only thing saved in the end was the customer's face, since the shrewd country merchant had anticipated this little ritual in pricing his goods. But it was a little game of wits that the buyers insisted upon, and it kept everybody happy.

Even among the sterling citizenry of the hills there would be an occasional crook who would bring the merchant what was presumably a mold of butter, but was, in reality, a clever facade. They would take cotton together with something to give weight and mold the exterior with enough butter to conceal the fraud and pawn it off on the store man as the genuine article. From there, it would be shipped to the dealer who, in turn,

30

would pass it on to the customer. Inevitably, about four weeks later, the merchant would catch merry hell. When he was able to track down the original culprit, he was in a unique position to properly penalize him without recourse to legal action.

One proprietor had a certain woman who wanted to sell her eggs and have them, too. It was her custom after she had sold her eggs, to steal them back when the merchant's back was turned, hiding them in her blouse, which could easily accommodate a dozen eggs. When he finally discovered her procedure one day, he casually approached her and announced warmly:

"Deanie, I think you are the most beautiful woman in the neighborhood, and I've always wanted to hug you."

With that he gave her a crushing embrace which at least broke her eggs if not her heart. I understand that this experience did not reform Deanie, but all agree it did discourage her.

The ability of the country store loafers as spitters was only exceeded by their capacity as gossipers. By comparison, the conversation at a Ladies' Aid gathering would seem harmless. They left no ground unturned and no subject was too sacred or too delicate for their examination. They hastened to rush in where no angel dared to tread. Between spits they piously pondered the lack of virtue among Skunk Hill women (a nearby den of iniquity), evaluated the virtue of their own wives, and bragged of their virility and their prowess with women. Naturally, the ones with the least boasted the loudest.

Occasionally, one of these fellows would exhibit a real flare for story-telling, and others developed reputations as local philosophers. There was one old fellow in particular who was quite a yarnster. He used to tell a story about a flight of passenger pigeons, which became extinct about the middle of the last century. He related the incident as his grandfather remembered, when reminiscing on the flight of these fowl. As he described it:

"They cum through by the hundreds of millions. When they roosted, they broke down the trees of the forest. They had a roosting place over on the east bank of the Greenbrier River, and when they settled down they would tilt the river right out of its banks. Grandpappy said that he saw them cum through once and there was a Hell's smidgin of 'em. They filled the skies and darkened the sun. They was so durned many of 'em that they filled up all the flyin' room in the air and a lot of 'em had to walk through.''

Though I have read many accounts of those fabulous flights, I have yet to find one to touch this one. Frankly, I think the Encyclopedia Brittanica should adopt this version instead of their usual one.

There was another of those fireside loafers who achieved a considerable reputation as a country philosopher. To his advantage, he even looked the part, being a tall man with a Lincoln profile and a Lincoln beard. In the hills, nothing will advance one's prestige as a philosopher faster than some resemblance to the immortal Lincoln. If anything, this man was even homelier that Lincoln, but his beard redeemed his appearance somewhat. Strangely enough, however, his wife was a strikingly beautiful woman. One day some "friend" was bold enough to inquire how his enchanting wife happened to marry one so ugly as himself. Rising to rare philosophic form, the man reasoned:

"Love is like lightening—it is just as apt to strike an outhouse as it is a palace.''

On another occasion, someone wondered why he wore a beard. In brilliant form, he responded:

"A beard is a thinking man's filter and a smoking man's firetrap.''

Since he was not a smoking man, that magnificent adornment must have served as his mental filter. People came from everywhere in the mountains to ask his advice. We had one young man in the community who was of more than average ambition, highly intelligent, and perhaps a little egotistical. He was firmly convinced that he would make his mark on the business world shortly. At the moment he was trying to make a decision whether to launch his career immediately or go to college and perhaps go even farther in the long run. After debating the matter pro and con for some time, he finally turned to the Philosopher for advice, emphasizing that quick success was his prime objective. The Philosopher wasted no time in counsel. Said he:

"Son, there are twenty formulas for quick success. The first is to marry a rich woman. The other nineteen don't amount to a damn.''

Oddly enough, the young man jumped at the idea, and married the only daughter of the richest man in the community. When the father-in-law died shortly thereafter, the young fellow inherited the business through his wife, and he quickly became the leading man in the community. Naturally, it enhanced the fame of our local Lincoln. Always thereafter his place at the Burnside stove was reserved as carefully as a seat at the stock exchange.

FIVE

MOUNTAIN COURTROOMS

Most trials were conducted either in the circuit court or, if not involving too much money or not too serious from the criminal standpoint, before a justice of the peace. Both were the scenes of many unusual happenings. I well remember one circuit court judge who, in my opinion, was utterly dedicated and honorable, but perhaps weighted a little more to the side of severeness than mercy. This was during the prohibition era, and even though West Virginia was the home of the great moonshiners of this region, it still was not the happiest thing to come before some of these mountain judges who had their own ideas on the subject.

On this particular occasion, the prosecuting attorney (who later was to be one of our congressmen) was a very fine lawyer who would prosecute vigorously when the occasion demanded, but also was inclined to be merciful if the situation so warranted. This was a liquor case and the defendant, in appearance at least, was the oldest man I have ever seen tried in a court room. He wore a long white beard and had a sad face lined with the deep wrinkles of age. The prosecuting attorney rose up and addressed the judge:

"Your Honor, this aged man pleads guilty to the manufacture of liquor or moonshine on his premises. However, it is my considered opinion that this man is more sinned against that having sinned. From all I can learn, his sons have taken advantage of his age and, against his wishes, have operated a still on the backside of his farm in a wooded section. Our officers, in raiding this still, failed to apprehend them but brought in this man who is the owner of the farm. Feeling that it is the general opinion of the community in which he lives that he is not the guilty one or ones, except through the technicality of owning the farm on which his sons operated the still, I as prosecuting attorney of this county am requesting Your Honor to be merciful to this aged man."

Looking toward the defendent, His Honor, in a kindly and respectful tone, spoke:

"Stand up, Mr. Oliver."

34

Mr. Oliver with effort stood up. In his kindly way His Honor continued:

"Our prosecuting attorney feels that in your case it is a matter of being more sinned against that having sinned and, in view of this fact and your extreme age, he has requested that I be merciful. I would like to say there is nothing I respect more than age, and I feel that the elderly people of this country have made their own significant contributions to our nation and state, enduring hardships that we have not known. So may I say to you, Mr. Oliver, that we will welcome you on your return. Two years in prison; may God speed you and the passing of the time."

Everyone was floored by this show of compassion, but the day was young and more was yet to come. The next case went like this:

A very young man was being tried for possession of a half pint of moonshine. He looked about high school age, and was a picture of the clean-cut All-American boy. Again the prosecutor rose and addressed the court:

"Your Honor, this young man is charged with the possession of a half pint of moonshine which the arresting officer found in his possession and which is present as evidence in this courtroom. It is true that we have suspected that this young man was engaged in selling liquor in the past, but actually we have no evidence of such act. He has no criminal record and this is his first appearance in court. In view of his youth, the fact that it is a first offense and that merely for the possession of moonshine rather than the manufacture or sale thereof, I will request that Your Honor be lenient and trust that this experience will be a lesson to this young man."

His Honor was equal to the occasion.

"Stand up, Mr. Crane," he instructed the defendant.

The young fellow rose. His Honor continued:

"Mr. Crane, you are a fine looking young man and our prosecutor feels that perhaps you will profit from this error. And in view of your youth and the fact that this is your first appearance in this court, he has urged that I be lenient. I wish to say that no one has a greater admiration for youth than myself. They are the brawn and brain of our great nation. It is they who are called upon to defend it. They are our future leaders. So we will welcome you on your return. Two years in prison."

With this second outburst of mercy, he adjourned court for

lunch as his last gracious gesture until the afternoon session that I was not privileged to attend.

Many times my father has told me a humorous incident which occurred while he was serving on a federal jury in a trial conducted by the late Judge Moore in Charleston. I don't remember what the case was all about. Whatever it was, one of his fellow jurors had managed to imbibe a little too much before reporting for duty. As the proceeding went on, this juror kept swaying forward in his seat as the witness on the stand was giving testimony and would cup his hand to his ear like he couldn't hear what the witness was saying. He probably couldn't, since he was pretty well lubricated. Finally, in the middle of everything he stood up, swaying on his feet, and announced to the judge:

"Your Honor (hic), I can't hear a word the witness says (hic), and besides, I think he is telling a damned lie anyhow!"

Judge Moore, who was a kindly soul not easily ruffled, took the whole thing in stride with the obvious solution.

"Mr. White," the Judge replied, "I believe we can excuse you from further duty." With that he started the trial all over again.

The real fun was in the Justice of the Peace courts. The typical Justice of the Peace was blissfully ignorant of law and proper legal procedure. Compounding the opportunities for injustice was the fact that in these courts the litigants often had to rely for counsel, not upon qualified attorneys, but some neighbor or jackleg legal "expert" who fancied himself a lawyer. It was a case of the blind dueling with the blind with a blind referee.

The story is told in the mountains—and I do not vouch for its accuracy—that old Squire Sydenstricker (all JP's were called "Squires") was trying his first case. It happened in this case that both litigants had lawyers. The plaintiff's counsel got up first and stated his case with eloquence unaccustomed in such proceedings. Overwhelmed by his logic, so convincingly presented, Squire Sydenstricker thought he had heard enough. Said he when the plaintiff's lawyer sat down:

"This case seems to be very clear and not open to any argument. In order to save time, I declare the verdict for the plaintiff."

Flabbergasted at this unorthodox procedure, the defense attorney jumped up and addressed the Squire:

"Your Honor, my client is entitled to have his side of the

36

case presented under due process of law, and in order that proper legal procedure may be followed, I would deeply appreciate it if you will at least let me present my client's case.''

Aware that the situation called for a herculean effort, the defense counsel mounted the pinnacle of his oratorical powers. His eloquence was equal to the occasion, for at the end of his presentation the amazed Squire moralized:

"This goes to show the wonderful power and majesty of the law. It proves that the law metes out justice with an unbiased hand. First the plaintiff wins. And now the defendant wins. Case decided in favor of the defendant.''

One of the more amusing trials in a JP court was the dog case tried before Squire Daniels. Lem Smith had Harry Hill in court, claiming that Harry's dog had come out on a country road and bit him. Both Lem and Harry had local talent representing them. Now some of these characters who tried to play Blackstone were at least ingenious, and Harry's got up and presented the case, trying with doubtful success to exhibit the scar on Lem's leg. This was hard to see, because of an accumulation of dirt on Lem's leg which awaited his annual spring bath.

Afterward, Harry's talent went to work. He began:

"Your Honor, and gentlemen of the jury. I have carefully questioned Mr. Hill relative to the incident in which his dog is alleged to have gotten loose, gone out on a public road, and to have bitten Lem Smith. I say it could not have happened, and I am going to ask you to find a verdict for Harry Hill for the following reasons:

"In the first place, Harry assures me that it would have been impossible for his dog to have gotten out to the country road because he has kept him at all times chained—with a very heavy chain—to a tree in his backyard.

"In the second place, even if he had gotten loose—which was impossible—the dog is a very gentle dog and wouldn't bite anyone.

"Furthermore, even if the dog had been so disposed to bite, that too would have been impossible because he is a very old dog and for the past year has not had a tooth in his head. Harry has had to keep him on mush and soft foods.

"And besides all this, gentlemen of the jury, Harry Hill does not even own a dog and never has owned a dog. His only possessions of this nature are five chickens and a cow. I am asking you to bring back a verdict in favor of my innocent client."

Without leaving the room, the jury returned the obvious verdict—not guilty.

There is another court story that must not go untold. It occurred far back in the hills about the turn of the century, in a circuit court proceeding. A judge told this incident which was supposed to have happened on his first trip to a certain county while he was still a fledgling jurist. Judges sometimes held court in several different counties, and I presume that is the reason they were (and still are in this state) called "circuit judges." It being his first visit to this particular county seat and each county having varying customs and procedures, the circuit clerk, just before court convened, led him to one side and informed him that for many years it had been a custom to open court with prayer by the Sheriff.

The new judge could see nothing wrong with this practice. So with all the potential jurors present, the judge took the bench and announced that the Sheriff would open with prayer in accord with the traditional custom. Now it so happened that the big trial for this term of court was the State versus Billy Bledsoe for the slaying of Hank Ellis. The Sheriff was equal to the task as he went right to work:

"Oh, God," he began, "we are gathered here to try that black-hearted murderer Billy Bledsoe for cold bloodedly and premeditatedly murdering Hank Ellis. We ask Thee, O God, to see that he pays on the gallows for this dastardly crime. We ask Thee to aid our prosecuting attorney in honing his mind and whetting his tongue so he may be able to circumvent the slick-tongued lawyers who will try to cloud and confuse the minds of the jury. We ask Thee to give our new judge upon the bench the wisdom and the will to instruct the jury in such a manner that there can be no loophole left for the sly counsel of this murdering scoundrel to get his case appealed. And, above all, we ask Thee, O God, to give wisdom and resolution to the hearts of this jury in order that they as jurors and citizens of this great state will do their duty and find this black-hearted Billy Bledsoe guilty of murder in the first degree. Amen."

The judge was utterly dumbfounded, but he did manage to remand Billy Bledsoe to jail for the next term of court and to enter an order that court hereafter be convened without the Sheriff's eloquent prayer.

SIX

THE MOUNTAIN CHURCHES

Most of the hill people were either Methodists or Baptists, and their spiritual needs were attended by circuit riding preachers who generally served at least four regular churches. This kept the preachers busy at a different church each Sunday of the month. In addition to these duties, there usually were some communities which used a school house for religious services, and the circuit riders would try to visit them as often as possible.

Helping to take up the slack, each community usually had a "one horse preacher" available. This was not necessarily a derogatory designation. In mountain idiom it could mean several things. It might imply merely that man was not ordained. Then it might simply indicate that he was not equipped with an extra horse when his regular saddler was lame or otherwise unable to travel. On the other hand, it often was used in a depreciatory sense, implying that the would-be preacher was not quite equal to the task.

In those days a man was not supposed to preach unless he was "called to preach." By this, people meant one had experienced the call of God. As a rule, the man who felt he was so called claimed that he received his call through an audible voice directing him to the task. Others claimed to have been called by means of night visions. Less sensationally, some merely saw or experienced something which they interpreted as a clear command to carry the message to their fellow man.

While hill people were innately religious and extremely emotional, this did not blind them to the shortcomings of their ministers. They could be sharply critical if they felt a preacher fell short of their standards. When a man did not measure up who claimed to have "the call," they could phrase their judgment of the individual expressively and pointedly. For example, if the would-be preacher was considered a lazy character who resorted to preaching to escape working, he was apt to be scorned as "a fugitive from the cornfield," an epithet which pretty well covered every shade of their opinion. When they were skeptical of a man's alleged call, they were liabel to wonder out loud if the preacher's "call" was perhaps "only an echo of his own voice, bounced back by the hill," or if maybe "he heard a bull frog croaking and thought it said 'go, preach! go preach!'"

Normally, however, they were as appreciative as they were religious and paid their preacher to the best of their ability. And when his circuit riding brought him to their church, he was always besieged with Sunday dinner invitations and even asked to spend the night if possible.

In the absence of refrigeration, the church family honored with the preacher's presence for Sunday dinner generally had to resort to the chicken yard for food. It got to the point that all the perennially mortal enemies of the chicken, such as the hawk, the eagle, and the big black snake, were considered bosom friends compared to the preacher. I can remember as a youngster hearing the chickens making a fuss and, thinking perhaps a hawk was after them, I would dash out to check on them. There they would be, looking down the lane in mortal terror. Sure enough, about a quarter of a mile away I would see our circuit riding minister heading our way. About then the chickens would start flying frantically for nearby trees, hoping desperately that Mother would pick a less fortunate fowl (and more convenient) which had not yet learned of the danger. In the end the mother hens spent more time training their biddies to fly and watch for the preacher than she did teaching them how to scratch for food. As refrigeration became more common, the chicken mortality rate increased and it became a more normal insurable risk. I will always believe that refrigeration meant more for chickens than it did for people. Of course, the preachers did well by it, too. For while chicken, gravy, and hot biscuits were real "good eatin," they did nothing for the minister as an insurance risk. I have observed since the advent of refrigeration that the average preacher's waistline is at least five inches smaller than his counterpart's in the heyday of chicken and hot biscuits forty years ago.

Ordinarily, our preachers were of two types: the Hell-Fire kind and the God-Is-Love variety. The majority were the Hell-Fire type, and these generally were considered more effective. Actually, many of these men were fairly good speakers who could paint a really fearsome picture with skillful words and back it up with Scripture point by point.

No lowlander could ever imagine or comprehend the revivals once held in our mountain communities. Fifty or so years ago,

40

for example, the men wore leggings and the women with their long hair wore an additional hair piece, known as a 'rat,' which was supposed to enhance the beauty of their natural hair. During revivals in my home church, I have seen men shouting until they lost their leggings and women carry on until the rats, pins and all, fell out of their hair. Wherever a preacher could spark such incidents, he was considered able and effective and consequently would be much in demand outside his own circuit.

Customarily, after a revival meeting had run its course, testimonial talks were given by those blessed during the services, including the new converts. These could occasionally lead to the most amusing incidents in spite of the spiritual surroundings or, perhaps, because of them. For instance, a neighbor of ours who was a rough logger, but a very fine fellow, "got religion" in one of these meetings and on his first Sunday after conversion, getting up to testify, began:

"My dear Christian friends, I'm so damned happy..."

Realizing suddenly that he was not in the log camp, he broke off in the middle of his words and sat down red-faced. It was several months before he regained enough composure to make another stab at it.

We had another neighbor, appropriately named Abraham, who was always good for a rousing testimonial. He was particularly enthusiastic after a stirring revival. After one such meeting he got up and passionately avowed that he could hardly wait to go to his reward in "that great Beulah land," meaning Heaven, of course. Later he evidently reversed his field, because when he became seriously ill shortly thereafter (he was about 50), he spent every dollar he had in order to stay here; he even mortaged his farm for the medical attention to prolong his earthly sojourn. He was still hanging on tenaciously until well up into his four score and ten, all of which shows how great it is to live in a country where one is free to change his mind about such things.

There was another neighbor who never missed a chance to testify. One of his testimonies was intriguing. Reminding the congregation of his recent misfortune, Hazle began:

"My friends, I guess you all know that some months ago my horse ran off, turning my wagon over with me under it, and I was hurt real bad. My back was injured, and simply wouldn't get well. Well, friends, I went to God with my problem and I promised Him that if He would heal me, I would always serve

Him. And you all know that my back isn't well yet."

With that baffling conclusion, Hazle sat down. No one quite knew whether Hazle was praising God or rebuking Him. To this day, people around there are still confused on that point.

One of the earliest tent meetings was held in eastern Greenbrier County (Asbury, W.Va., if I recall correctly). The tent was rather large and the evangelist was quite a spell-binder who attracted sizeable crowds. He would invite people to come to the altar whereupon he would proceed to ask "Jesus to come down" right then and there. He actually seemed to be asking Jesus to appear physically instead of spiritually. There happened to be a local school teacher in attendance who had a little larceny in his veins. Wondering what would happen if 'Jesus' physically appeared, he arranged for an answer. So on a later night when the evangelist was making his customary request for Jesus to come, suddenly there appeared in the door of the tent a small white mule ridden by a figure clothed in white. Pandemonium broke loose as the congregation tore the sides out of the tent in their haste to flee, with the itinerant evangelist well in the forefront of his closest competitors.

The embarrassed evangelist was so enraged at the mischevious school teacher, who had put a large student up to the hoax, that he tried to get the prosecuting attorney to issue a warrant for the school teacher for disturbing public worship. The prosecutor refused on the grounds that worship was only disturbed because the evangelist thought at the time he was getting what he asked for. This story appeared several times in the *West Virginia News* and was verified by Judge Dice who, I think, was the prosecuting attorney.

Most of our preachers, however, were sincerely dedicated men of God who labored heroically in the vineyard. Their gruelling circuits required much wearisome horseback riding and their monetary reward was rarely in line with their labors. They smote the Devil hip and thigh, seven days a week. To have survived such unceasing warfare, the Devil proved himself at least a durable old bird. Yet to the mountain preachers, two accomplishments can be safely attributed: they powerfully restrained the forces of sin, and they greatly reduced the chicken population.

As suggested earlier, frequently persons felt called to preach who were academically unqualified for the job. Even though the educational requirements for ordination in those days were

42

usually pretty low, some men who attempted to preach fell woefully short of the minimal standards that did exist. However, they did not let this discourage them. They became "exhorters" and held their meetings wherever chance would allow them without the license or the blessing of the Conference Board or any other ecclesiastical agency.

There was a certain one of these unlicensed preachers who was endowed with an impressive appearance and a deep, melodious voice that could rattle the rafters. But he was severely handicapped by his inability to read. To a less determined and resourceful fellow, this would have proved an insurmountable obstacle, but for this man it was only an aggravation. To redeem the situation, he was always accompanied in his itinerary by his nephew, who had "book larnin'." Their system called for the young to always stand directly behind his uncle and whisper the words as his uncle "read" to his congregation from his Bible with his impressively resonant voice. One particular Sunday morning the pair took the rostrum with the nephew standing dutifully back of his uncle's shoulder, as his whispering hope. Announced the uncle to the congregation:

"My text today will be the thirty-fourth chapter of the book of Exodus."

Then, with the nephew whispering helpfully, the preacher began to read, his voice ringing with emotion:

"The Lord said unto Moses..."

Unfortunately, his thumb was covering the next word, so the nephew whispered frantically:

"Move your thumb!"

"...move your thumb!" the preacher continued dramatically. Even this devout and reverent mountain audience almost broke up the service with laughter.

The most amusing church incident I ever witnessed occurred in 1917 at the Buckhorn Church in Snow Hill, West Virginia. At the time I was rooming in my uncle's store at Hominy Falls. We had there a circuit rider by the name of Goff. Being a little more polished than the average country preacher, we regarded him as something of a city-slicker. In fact, he did come from Charleston, which is the state capital and was our second largest city.

Reverend Goff on this occasion was holding revival services in the neighboring Buckhorn community. Since the only place to meet girls around there was at church, I became an inveterate church-goer, and that is how I happened to be attending these services. One Saturday night, after a full week of meetings and disappointing results, we found Reverend Goff quite distressed. He frankly acknowledged to the congregation that the revival had not progressed satisfactorily and chided them for being "cold and indifferent." He added that if things did not warm up tonight, he felt it would be wise to terminate the meetings. Then he announced that he was going to read his text, bring his message, and then invite anyone who felt the need to come to the altar while the choir sang "a good ol' fashioned hymn" in one last grand and glorious effort to warm everybody up.

He really lit into his sermon, preaching with fervor and rare eloquence, at the conclusion of which he extended the altar invitation and requested the choir to come forth with a good old religious song while people made their way to the front.

This choir was undoubtedly one of the most unusual groups ever assembled in the history of Christianity. I would be cheating posterity if I did not describe the appearance of these singers. Since all of them, so far as I know, are still living, I will not use their names.

The "Choir" consisted of three of the motliest looking men that ever embarrassed the face of the earth. One was a scrawny, rat-faced fellow weighing about 110 pounds. The second was likewise, about the size of a large flake with droopy eyelids, while the third was simply nondescript. I knew the three of them personally and can say with complete assurance that if one had hunted from the Virginia line to the Pennsylvania border, three more ignorant fellows could not have been found.

By the time they had completed their performance, one person at least was visibly warmed—the Reverend Goff. Instead of singing a good old religious hymn as the Reverend had requested, they sang a song about a Louisiana planter on his death bed. It seems he had gone fox-hunting and developed swamp fever. As he lay on his death-bed, he called for his true love to come to his bedside, where he expressed his eternal love for her and requested that she put a turtle dove at the head and foot of his grave to show he died for love.

They had copied the poem on a narrow piece of tablet paper out of *Hearth And Home* magazine, a popular publication in those days which always ran a page or two of poetry. There they stood, whining and whanging away, blissfully unaware that it was about as unappropriate for the occasion as "Buffalo Gals" or "The Shy Young Maid from Armitieres." Unwarned and unprepared for such impropriety, the Reverend glared at them with astonishment and dismay bordering on a state of shock.

The entertainment had just begun. When they got to the third verse, discovering they had mislaid it and had the tablet pages out of proper order, they began frantically turning the pages. At last they found it and started all over, to the horror or Reverend Goff. As it happened, in their fumbling they had gotten the pages more disorganized than ever, requiring them, moments later, to stop again. By this time, the Reverend had begun to pace the floor nervously, his hands clenched into a sweaty fist and each step seemed to be a curse. That he was a much disturbed man was apparent to all but the choir, which was preoccupied with finding the proper page of poetry, which they were "singing" without the benefit of music and, so far as I could tell, without a tune, happy in the notion that they were bringing to the congregation one of the all-time great sacred renditions. It never entered their feeble minds that Reverend Goff only by the greatest effort was restraining himself from commiting mayhem. Finally, when he could endure it no longer, Reverend Goff, as he fretfully paced the floor, burst in with "Jesus, Lover of My Soul" in a voice that sounded strangely like swearing.

On that sour note he closed the Buckhorn revival.

I left the church wondering if perhaps the next county paper would report that Reverend Goff had been charged with manslaughter or possibly let off with a ruling of justifiable homicide. However, nothing appeared and, since I later saw the singers, it was evident the Reverend Goff's basic emotions gave in to his Christian upbringing.

45

SEVEN

THE MOUNTAIN DOCTOR

The early mountain doctors evoke a sense of nostalgia. Like the circuit riding preachers, these old-time physicians were a dedicated breed of men who took seriously their Hippocratic Oath and seldom allowed Hell or high water to interfere with their visitations of mercy.

Unlike their modern counterparts who as frequently as not conjure up to their patients shades of highway bandits, the early mountain doctors labored with the humanitarian spirit of latter-day Good Samaritans.

These men faithfully tended the needs of their widely scattered patients in the face of tremendous adversity. They made their seemingly endless rounds on horseback to the remotest places. Day and night the early mountain doctor went through snow, hail, sleet and hazards of every description to relieve human suffering. When he couldn't travel horseback, he walked where he could, surmounting mountainous snow drifts and fording high waters. The so typical indifference of the modern doctor is ample evidence to me that all change is not necessarily to be equated with progress.

A comfortable living was due such men and usually they made one, but not unreasonably so. I suspect our contemporary physicians spill more money on the way to the bank than our doctors made in a month. If his patients did not have money for his services, the doctor waited—many times in vain—and sometimes he settled for beef, butter, and eggs or other farm products.

It was unfortunate that the remedies of these early mountain doctors fell somewhat short of their dedication. In this respect, medicine has come a long way even if its character has deteriorated. The old practitioners had a prejudice for calomel and caster oil on which occasions the thinking man's patient was careful to have an option on the nearest outhouse. These were potent remedies and were some gauge of the constitution of survivors who could be considered thereafter worthy tests of the cruelest plagues known to mankind.

As you might expect, some of these old timers were as

46

colorful as they were committed. There was once a doctor in our community who was considerate of the poor and charged reasonably for his services, but was notoriously frugal with his receipts. He clung to a penny as tenaciously as life itself. When he finally died, many local people were sure he had managed to take it all with him or he wouldn't have gone. In life, however, he and my father were members of the local Odd Fellows Lodge. Just for fun, my father one day started a petition to get Doc a new suit to replace the shabby one he perennially wore with dubious distinction. Doc, of course, could have bought and sold any three members of the Lodge. Shortly, Doc got word of the mock petition and sometime later he met my father.

"Watson," he inquired, "I understand that some of you down at the Lodge are taking up money to buy me a suit of clothes." Father confessed discussing the subject.

"It's a good idea," Doc confided; "I'll go a dime on it myself."

Sometimes the mountain patient was as colorful as his physician. One of my acquaintances was a coal doctor most of his life, and he once told of his most memorable experience in medicine.

The doctor at the time was a company physician and had gone to deliver the baby of the wife of Zeb Stone, a miner. As he entered the home, Zeb was sitting before the fireplace staring stoically at the crackling flames. He uttered a cheerful greeting which Zeb did not acknowledge. In fact, he didn't even raise his head or seem to observe his entrance. It was a large room, which served as both living room and bedroom for the entire family. Off in one corner was Mrs. Stone, in labor. In another corner were two young children down with measles; and sitting in a nearby chair was an early-teenage daughter, who herself looked suspiciously pregnant. He noticed Zeb also had his leg in a cast, and he recalled that only about two weeks before it had been broken in a slate fall. The doctor hastened to his business and delivered a squalling eight-pound boy. Zeb had not yet spoken a single word when the doctor was preparing to leave. So he walked over to Zeb, who was already the father of nine children, and made the completely unnecessary announcement that Zeb was a father again. That did it.

"Doc," Zeb inquired, "do you read the Good Book?"

The doctor assured Zeb that he occasionally read the Bible.

"Don't it say, Doc, that a man shall not be burdened with

47

more than he can bear?'' Zeb asked.

The doctor confirmed that it did.

"Doc, don't you think I'm bein' pushed jist a mite?"

EIGHT

WHAT A MAN!

Without doubt one of the most intriguing men ever to inhabit these hills has to be Guy D. Holbrook, a man for whom I once worked. My brother several years ago suggested to Adrian Gwin of the *Charleston Daily Mail* that Holbrook would make a good subject for a human interest feature. Mr. Gwin got right on it and did a fine double installment feature on this unusual man which appeared in the *Mail* on May 31 and June 4 of 1962. With Mr. Gwin's gracious permission, here is the Guy Holbrook story as it appeared in the paper:

(May 31
Roving the Valley--Greenbrier man cures broken leg unassisted
By Adrian Gwin of the Daily Mail Staff

The telephone voice was positive:
"He set his broken leg himself. He laced the leg into a high-top boot, nailed the boot to the floor, and then sat there for 18 days while the leg healed!"
I doubted it. "Baloney!" I said.
But, where there's fire, there's smoke, I figured.
I determined to find Guy D. Holbrook and prove or disprove this fantastic-sounding yarn.
"Where does this character live?" I asked.
"He lives 'way out, two or three miles from anywhere, up the Meadow River in Greenbrier County."
"A hermit?" I asked.
"Call him that if you like. He has lived completely alone for 14 years."
"How old is he?"
"Up in his 80's, I think."

EASY TO MISS RUSSELVILLE
I thanked the man after getting some more information about this fellow who used a boot for a cast, and I headed up U.S. 60 to Lookout and beyond, where Rt. 19 takes off northward toward Summersville.
Instead of making that wide sweeping curve right at the junction, I kept straight on, onto 19, and drove three miles to the village of Russelville.
You can be in and out of it and far up the road before you even see the town if you miss the sign pointing off to the right: "Russelville Post Office."
I crossed the wooden bridge and the railroad tracks with the sign

49

"NF&GRR"—the Nicholas Fayette and Greenbrier—and stopped at the post office beside the red-dog and gravel road.

Postmaster Janice Burr laughed out loud when I asked directions to Guy Holbrook's home.

"You'll have to walk, but he walks it all the time," she said, pointing up the tracks where a diesel engine was coasting down from the wilds of Greenbrier County, a string of hopper cars full of wood chips following along behind.

Clyde Haynes, a retired contractor, came in to mail a letter and he listened. "Get him to tell you about the time they undertook to put him in jail up at Rainelle!" said Clyde. "He was younger then, and he got disorderly or something, and he took on just about the whole town. He told me long afterward, 'I never thought It'd be so much fun to fight a crowd!

" 'When you hit one, you can knock a whole bunch of 'em down!' he said.

WAS POWERFUL IN YOUNGER DAYS

"And I understand they never did get him in jail. He was a powerful man in his youth, a man that never lost the humor of a situation, no matter what came. He could fight with a smile on his face."

Janice Burr said "He used to make a lot of ax-handles, and then he'd walk miles to sell 'em. He still makes a few things out of wood, but his left hand is partly paralyzed from a stroke last year and he can't work as fast as he used to."

When the train got through switching into the asphalt plant siding there, I parked the car by the railroad and started walking up the tracks.

The Meadow River tumbles down from the mountains and runs beside the railroad, and as I walked the ties I felt very much like a boy playing hookey. It was all I could do to keep from stripping and diving into a quiet green pool where the water swirls lazily around a boulder the size of a six-room house.

A Cooper's hawk sailed across the river and glided noiselessly 10 feet over my head. The railroad tracks stretched a mile ahead, and curved away in the sunshine as I stepped from tie to tie, wondering how in the world an 80-year-old man ever manages to carry his groceries home by walking the tracks.

At the white cottage in a clearing beside the railroad I noticed a newly built footbridge across the ditch. The front steps were gone, and rye-grass was growing porch-high in the front, but the path went around back, so I went too.

A half-wild dog leaped out of the lilac bushes and barked himself off into the brush up the hill.

I stopped beside the house and hollered "Hey, Mr. Holbrook!" and waited for any answer.

COVERED BY GUN IN HOUSE APPROACH

There was a beehive on the front porch, and another on the back porch by the kitchen door. A third hive was housed by the bedroom window, in a wooden barrel with the staves split down one side, where the bees went in and out. There were four other beehives in the yard.

I thought "It's a fine day for the bees," for there were thousands of the little fellows zooming across the yard in three or four "beelines." Plenty of clover and flowers blooming, and those bees were making the most of it.

I called again. The back door was open and I knew he must be home. Then

50

I heard a gentle bump inside. Something had been dropped to the floor. (I learned later it was the 12-guage shotgun which had been covering me from the bedroom window.)

Guy Holbrook, dragging his left leg only slightly, appeared at the door.

"Come in! Come in!" he said, in a hearty voice. I introduced myself, and he made me sit in his worn old rocking chair while he took the straight chair by the window.

Briefly, I outlined to him the story I'd heard about his broken leg in a boot nailed to the floor. "Is that true?" I asked him point-blank.

His yellow-white hair reminded me of Robert Frost's pictures. And his face looked sort of cherubic as he smiled an answer.

"It was a lot worse than that!" he said.

(Don't miss Guy D. Holbrook's first-person "brief biography of myself" that he told to the Roving Reporter, next Monday in "Roving the Valley.")

June 4--roving the valley
guy holbrook lives alone and likes it--by adrian gwin of the daily mail staff

I'd driven 75 miles and walked about three miles to get to the isolated home of Guy D. Holbrook.

We were in his bedroom beside the railroad tracks up the Meadow River from Russelville, and I was questioning him about his colorful and adventure-filled life.

"He won't tell you a thing, maybe, and then again if he takes a liking to you, he might tell you things we haven't found out in 40 years of neighboring with him," they'd said at the post office.

Mr. Holbrook must have taken a liking to me.

"Now young feller, you've asked me, and I just believe I'll give you a brief biography of myself, if you want me to," the white-haired old gentleman said.

He packed his pipe and scratched a country match across the top of the cold Warm Morning stove, leaned back and puffed, while I grabbed for my pencil.

"First I want you to know that I've read the Bible through 63 times, and never skipped a page or a verse ary a time.

"That time I broke my leg, it was the 22nd day of March two years ago, and a cold day with snow on the ground, you remember.

WENT OUT-OF-DOORS TO LOOSEN MUSCLES

"I'd set in the house a-readin' my Bible and I got stiff in the shoulders. Thinks I to myself I'll just go out and loosen up my muscles a little. I took that 14-pound sledge and stepped out near the shed-house and just swung a couple of licks at a big flat rock, when I saw that bolt.

"It was a five-eights bolt, five inches long, and it seemed to me that with a point on it, it would just fit the eye of an axe. I laid down the 14-pound hammer and put the bolt on it, and swung with an eight pound hammer to beat a point on it.

"On the third lick, it spun away and went point-on right through my left leg, half-way between the knee and the ankle.

"I fell like a pole-axed ox, all of a heap. When I come to I could see the

51

bolt-head, and my leg was turned back sideways, and the blood was a'gushin'.

"With my fingers I pulled the bolt out, and then I passed out again and when I come to again, I knew I had to get into the house."

(Guy Holbrook has lived alone for 14 years, more than 2 miles away from the nearest other person.)

"I've studied some medicine myself, don'tcha see, for my father was a noted physician, Isaac Winfree Holbrook. I was born in Lawrence County, Ky., of a big family. There were nine children of us, three girls and six boys.

"Yes, the broken leg. Well, sir, I tore up an old stave basket and bound up the leg with the parts, and tied them with bailing wire and then I got the haft of a cant hook, without the hook, you know, and used it for a splint, and got inside.

LIVED WITH LAST WIFE FOR 34 YEARS

"No, I didn't set the leg in a boot and nail it to the floor. I'll tell you what I did. I nailed four nails around my shoe, and set bricks around my foot to hold it in place while I set it. First I had to take out six pieces of the splintered bone, which I did, though Lord! how weak I was.

"There was a long splinter that went further than the hole on either side, and it was loose and I knew it had to come out. I thinks to myself, I'll just get a razor and split the leg.

"And don'tcha know—I lost my nerve!

"But I boiled it out with peroxide and I kept it open for many a long week until it all healed from the inside. Never an infection did it get and all the medicine I used was peroxide and camphophenol, that I put great store by, you see.

"It was a job, setting the leg and binding that cant hook handle to it for a brace, and four months I was getting it well enough for me to walk, but see now, how straight it is, though you can see the scar." (There was a scar about the size of a silver dollar over the shin-bone as the old man pulled up his pants leg to show.)

"I was about 13 when my father moved to West Virginia. We'd moved from Kentucky to down near Birmingham, Ala., and to Virginia and then to Webster County.

"When I was about 18 there was a girl I'd set out to marry, Laura Donaldson she was, 17 and a beautiful girl.

"I'd come into an $800 inheritance when my mother died, and I jumped at it and bought me a house and a farm and 24 hogs, eight cows, four horses and some other things.

GIRL FATALLY HURT IN FALL

"While I was in town gettin' the license she fell out of a cherry tree and received her death wounds. I found her like that when I got back with the license. She wanted to go ahead with the wedding and we did, she on her death-bed. She died four days later and I was a wild man, I tell you.

"I left the country and went down to Kentucky and I wasn't no angel, I tell you. But in some months I met a girl named Annie Osborn—she was a wonderful woman!

"To make it short, I married her, lived with her for a year or so, until the eighth month of her pregnancy. She got—and mind you, I'm not saying a thing against the girl—she got cross-tempered and quarrelsome with everything. I stood it and stood it when she turned on me, and on my father, but when she called my mother a slut I left her, and our baby unborn as yet.

"I never got no divorce from her, no, I just left her. She had the baby and he's still living in Lawrence County, Ky., 58 years old now with grandchildren of his own, so I'm a great-grandfather, don't you see!

"Well I went to Birmingham and there I met a wonderful woman, so sweet and like an angel, a church worker and all that, and after a while I married her.

"But she had spoken with a forked tongue and had deceived me, I learned, so I got that marriage annulled and I went off to Arkansas where I lived with an older brother for a while.

"It was there that I met Kate Pendergrass, a half-breed Indian girl, in Woodruff County. Kate was the prettiest thing you ever saw and so jolly and full of fun!

"We got married, Kate and I, she with her coal black hair and sparkling black eyes, she was within a half inch of being as tall as I was, the best-humored thing that ever drawed a breath!

"I lived with her 10 months and she never made me a meal in that time. She wouldn't cook! Laugh all the time, but never cook a meal, and I tired of that. I pulled out from there and catched a boat, the John K. Speed and made my upriver to Charleston, W.Va..

"Kate died in the course of time, I heard, but I'll never forget her.

"I walked 77 miles to Savage Town on Strange Creek, and on into Webster County, and I took a contract. I ketched a fine job cutting logs. A fellow by the name of Lee Gadd went in with me to cut the logs, and I had a woods crew of fine Americans. We worked so hard and made so much money the fellow I worked for aimed to make me quit.

"It was near Tioga, in Webster County, and they aimed to get the bohunks in and the Americans out. They got a hundred bohunks and they fired on us in the night. We went out and bought a Winchester and a high-powered Savage and two Colt's pistols and plenty of ammunition.

"On the second night after that, here they come! You could hear the bullets whistlin' over the camp-shacks.

"I said fellows, we ain't going to waste an ounce of powder nor throw away a ton of lead. And we crept out and got right close to them and we fired over a hundred shots there.

"If you ever seen turkeys scatter through the woods that's the way it was that night. The boss sent word the next day that he was a peaceful man and that he would sign a contract to get rid of all the bohunks, and, by gosh, he did!

"I want you to know that I didn't marry again for 12 years after I left Kate, and then I married a Pennsylvania woman, Adeline Good, that I met in Webster County. We were married on the 26th of April, in 1914, and I lived with her for 34 years and four days. She died on the 30th day of April in 1948.

"She was honestly the best reader I ever heard, and had the sweetest voice! She could spell the spelling book through and not miss a word!

"I've had five women in my life, but since she died, I've stayed right here and never have showed the least sign of wanting another woman. Nobody has ever fried me an egg, boiled me a potato nor so much as opened me a can of pork and beans. I've done it all myself for 14 years.

"Now son, it was some time after I cured my broken leg that I walked into Russelville and Sarah Collins at the grocery store asked of my health. I told her that I felt numb in my feet. I met Chloe Haynes and she said I ought to soak my feet in hot water. I got on home, and went right to bed.

"When I waked up, I was paralyzed in my left side. I couldn't move. I rolled out of bed onto the floor and laid there 24 hours before I could get up.

"I was always a fellow to laugh at hardship, and I remember laughing as I thought 'I cured my leg to come to this!'

"For 22 days I never spoke to a soul, and the last eight days I was out of food and going on to starve. I got a rope and tied up my left leg in a sling and took a stick and dragged myself up the path and two miles out to the road.

"I hired me a car and went to Russelville and got a good supply of groceries and had 'em hauled—and me with 'em—back here to my house. Not a bit of medicine did I ever take except that which I fixed for myself, and today I can walk pretty good for an old man. Old? I'll be 80 years old on July the 29th, if the Lord spares me to then.

"The NF&G? No sir! That's the Sewell Valley Branch of the C&O Railroad, young man! The section crews—and it's mighty nice of the company to let them do it for me—bring me my groceries now on the motorcars. Ray Short drops my mail off to me and I hired him to paint my place a little, but I built that bridge out there myself, carried all those timbers and boards and built it alone I did.

"I'd be delighted you'd take a picture of me! Let me put on a clean shirt. Here, I'll show you something." His bright blue eyes shone as he unwrapped a quilt on the sofa in the little living room, and revealed a battered violin.

"I'm an old-time fiddler, yes sir! I've heard 'em all on the radio and not one of 'em can fiddle to suit me. I can't either, not anymore, since my stroke, for my left hand has no strength in it for the strings.

"Stay a while and I'll fix us something to eat. Just got my groceries this morning. You walking back? Yes, it's two miles. It's exactly two miles and nine of those 33-foot rail lengths from my gate to the front of the post office in Russelville.

"I'd be proud you'd stay a while longer."

Over his shoulder I could see the barrel of that 12-guage shotgun, standing beside the bed, and in his hands was the tattered old Bible which he had read from cover to cover 63 times.

What a man!

NINE

THE MOST UNUSUAL POST OFFICE

The post office in our community was virtually a family heirloom. It was named after my great grandfather and was housed in his home. It remained in our family until about 1934, when it was discontinued, having fallen a victim to the star route system which replaced many rural post offices.

When my father and mother were married, he purchased the old homeplace where she was born and thus inherited the community post office. In those days politics was not as much involved in the postal system as today, and it was possible for him to be appointed postmaster without bringing every political hack from Nutterville to Washington in on the act.

Never in all the years my father was postmaster was our house locked, and this obviously meant that the post office incorporated in the home was never locked either. After the original homeplace burned in 1913, father built a new home: a large, two-story white house with four bedrooms, with a special large hall-type room to accommodate the post office. If we were out on the farm or perhaps attending church when a neighbor needed postal service, it was a normal practice for them to walk in, help themselves, and leave the correct change, if any.

This procedure was challenged about 1915, with the descent of the first postal inspector on the community. We had admirably survived well over a half a century without an inspector, but this particular fellow—it seems to me his name was White—probably felt that since he was inspector, he must inspect in the sacred tradition of the postal book. In any case, when he arrived at our community and inquired about the location of the post office, he was pointed to our place. It was a beautiful day in the early fall, and the family was dispersed on the rangy farm. After no one answered his knocks, the inspector ventured inside the open door into what he discovered to his dismay was the post office, unlocked and unattended. He opened the stamp drawers and before him were stamps, money, and in fact about all the articles that make up a post office. For a postal inspector, he was understandably flabbergasted at such unorthodox and, to him, irresponsible management. As he was surveying the scene Father and Mother came in, to whom he quickly introduced himself. Without fanfare he proceeded with all the zeal of a bureaucratic Barney Fife to dress down my father, describing the situation as the most "shocking" in all his years as a postal inspector. He deplored the operation of this post office as not only "illegal," but also "irresponsible." So grave a matter would compel him to turn in an unfavorable report and it was quite possible, the inspector advised Father, that he would be severely reprimanded by the postal department and perhaps even removed from his position.

With such people my father was not given to patience. An articulate man, he wasted no time returning the inspector's indiscriminate fire with a withering blast of indignation, seasoned with choice profanity. With impressive style, Father informed the unprepared inspector that his house had never been locked in so many years and advised him, moreover, that it was never going to be locked, come Washington or high water. What is more, he continued with measured arrogance, he kept the post office only for his own convenience and for that of his neighbors. During his tenure, the inspector was reminded with considerable vigor, there had never been a single shortage and even if there should be, he, be it understood, was good for it. Finally, if his operational procedures were unacceptable to Mr. White and his superiors, he could take his rinky-dink post office and "get the hell back to Washington with it."

At first the inspector seemed stunned by such a commanding counterattack, and then apparently realizing that the post office was in good hands even when it seemed to have no hands or perhaps that his passion was greater than the stakes, he abruptly changed the subject and began to admire the magnificent virgin timber he saw on the way in and inquire about the hunting. Father, who could get on a mad spell with the bat of an eye, could get over one in half that time. Suddenly a paragon of cordiality and rural hospitality, he assured the inspector that the hunting in that vicinity was excellent and that if he wished to stay over and hunt, he would furnish him with all the necessary equipment except a license, an item no one except city slickers bothered about.

Mr. White eagerly accepted his invitation and Father, who could charm a bird off a limb when he was so disposed, showed him such hospitality that for many years thereafter Mr. White returned during hunting season to check the post office that was never locked. Afterward, he claimed that he had told the story of our little post office at many postal conventions and so far as any of his counterparts knew, it was the only one of its kind in existence.

TEN

THE GREAT TIMBER ERA

Around the turn of the century, West Virginia was victimized by the voracious greed of the lumber industry.

Taking no thought for tomorrow, these selfish men descended on every tract of timber on which they could get a toehold and began the brutal rape of our state's virgin forests, representing what was then the finest growth of diversified hardwood on the surface of the earth. The lumber industry went after timber like it was going out of style with callous disregard for scientific procedure. Instead of discrimanately removing older and larger trees to make room for the new growth and thereby conserving their beauty and prosperity for countless tomorrows, the timber tycoons had eyes only for the dollar of the day. Unfortunately, there was no one in government or private life with the foresight or perhaps courage to raise a voice of protest against this shameful waste of natural resources. So, for years there was a "thunder in the mountains," and the only voice was one crying in the wilderness, "T-I-M-B-E-R!" That great cry of the timber cutter echoed thousands of times each day across the forests as the timbermen fed the insatiable appetite of the big band saws. Many of these lumbermills would cut up to one hundred thousand feet of timber a day, and there were dozens of them cutting simultaneously across the state.

But for the mountaineer there were some benefits in this invasion. Almost overnight, boom towns would be created far back in the hills and with them came a prosperity hitherto unknown to the hillbilly. He could now sell for cash all the farm products he could raise, and if he desired, he could go to work for the lumber company.

Timbering went on ten hours a day, five and a quarter days a week, with no letup. When the woodhicks got paid, these mountain towns were the scenes of blowouts that would make the antics of the Wild West look tame by comparison, except for the fact that the woodhicks were armed with bare (in some cases, *bear*) fists instead of guns. When he was sober, the ordinary woodsman was a stout-hearted, well-met fellow who would give a person in need the shirt off his back. When he was drunk, however, he was as different as Dr. Jekyll and Mr. Hyde. He turned from a good-natured giant into a fearsome, raging beast who fought at the drop of a hat or less—usually less. To him, fighting was fun and his consummate joy was to flatten a town. More reasonable than the average woodhick, but a man with an almost legendary capacity for drunken violence, was the notorious Bob Guthrie, who was finally killed about 1920 not far from Sewell Mountain. When Bob worked for the Cherry River Boom and Lumber Company, he would come into Richwood for his fun. There he would get drunk and sack out on a restaurant table to sleep it off. The routine was often the same after that. The indignant proprietor would finally threaten to call the local law. Being a tractable man who would never break a law so long as it was convenient to obey it, Bob would attempt to discourage any rash action that might precipitate any unpleasantness. That would be most foolish, Bob would explain impassionately, since by calling the law he would be forced to resist arrest and this would mean the owner's establishment would be hopelessly wrecked. If it came to this, he promised to break out the front windows and personally shatter all the glassware before he was over-powered. As his credentials for destructive power were well established, the proprietors of his favorite habitats found him quite persuasive, as a rule. Woe betide the exceptions!

Another notable representative of this breed was big Tom O'Dell, a fighting demon, but later one of the finest sheriffs in the history of Nicholas County. Then there were the rowdy McClung brothers who fought outsiders when they could, fought each other when they couldn't—and heaven pity the poor devil who made the mistake of taking sides when they were infighting only to have them all turn on him. The economic advantages of tolerating the woodhick on payday helped the mountain business community to adjust to these men and their destructive, fighting proclivities. He was a man who lived as if there was no tomorrow—which was often the case, as his was a reckless, dangerous life.

Too late West Virginians learned that when the reaping is done, the fields are bare. Worse yet, we awakened to the reality that unlike fields, great forests do not grow back the next year, but like most things of great value, they take time to come by. What the lumber companies in their wanton avarice did not destroy, fire did. The tree tops left in the wake of a cutting left thousands of acres of smaller timber at the mercy of a careless match. Little wonder that forest fires devoured the leavings of a priceless heritage that our state sold for a mess of pottage. Much of that fabulous timber brought less per acre in those days that a mere twelve-inch plank would bring in the modern market. I can remember when top grade oak flooring sold for thirty dollars per thousand. Today flooring of that same quality is unattainable at any price. Lumber considered first class nowadays was used back then to build pig pens.

In fact, much that is considered premium lumber today would have been completely culled in the great timber era.

The ravage of the forests had its repercussions on other natural resources. Unfortunately, most of the sawmills were situated along many beautiful streams, where sawdust and acid polluted the waters.

It is a tragedy that my generation and the preceding one did not have the vision to safeguard our heritage. Today, West Virginia is not even a reasonable facsimile of its former natural splendor.

Only in a land unspoiled by greedy men can great forests grow.

ELEVEN

THE LOGGING RAILROADS

For the benefit of railroad buffs, note should be taken of the old logging trains.

The ravage of our virgin mountain forests was a gigantic operation sprawling from the Cheat and Yew Pine mountains on the north and east to New River and the gorges of lower Gauley River on the south and west.

A few of the more prominent logging companies operating in our vicinity were the Meadow River Lumber Company of Rainelle, the Wilderness Lumber Company of Nallen, the Cherry River Boom and Lumber Company of Richwood, and the Pardee and Curtin Lumber Company of Curtin and Hominy Mills.

These outfits gave rise to some of the boldest and most bizarre railroading in the annals of the business. Every type of engine imaginable was used to transport timber from its barely accessible mountain forests to the mills—Shay engines, side-wheelers, mallards, and every other rail-running contraption that could operate by steam. Some ran on standard guage tracks; others used narrow gauge tracks; and I am not sure that occasionally they did not run without any tracks at all.

The life of a logging railroader was hazardous. This was particularly true of the Pardee and Curtin crews, whose trains used narrow gauge tracks on scandalously bad roadbeds. A fine day it was when at least one of their trains didn't run off. Most times this occurred as the trains attempted to scale the grudging sides of imposing mountains by the use of switchbacks, or on downhill stretches where their brakes failed. The runaway trains often derailed, bringing occasional death and frequent injury to its crew, which generally survived these experiences by a hasty exit from the stampeding train. Precarious as his occupation was, the typical railroader took all its dangers in stride and wouldn't have traded jobs with his congressman.

I recall one Pardee and Cartin engineer who rode out a near disaster with typical aplomb. Just before the accident he had visited my uncle's store in Hominy Falls, where he purchased a ham of meat and a dozen eggs. He put the eggs in his dinner pail, whisked up the meat with his free hand, and returned to his log train. Later that day on the way back to Curtin the train derailed into the Gauley River, completely submerging the cab in water. The engineer reportedly emerged from the window of his buried cab with his bucket of eggs—undoubtedly broken—in one hand and his ham of meat in the other, standing knee-deep in water covering his engine and bellowing, "Where the hell is the fireman?!" The incident was undoubtedly true, since the bystanders who reported the incident to us would have had no knowledge that those two items were in the engineer's possession.

Other companies did not have nearly so many of these accidents, but railroading for any log road was never at any time a life for the faint-hearted.

The grades on which these railroads were laid out would have caused a civil engineer to bite his slide rule. For many years the General Woods Superintendent laid out the path of Meadow River Lumber Company railroad. To say that his grades were the best in our section of the state is only a commentary on the incredibility of the others.

I always believed, for example, that Pardee and Curtin put their railroads exactly where whims would have them, not where the caprice of Mother Nature might receive them. Some of those incredible grades which would be considered impossible by modern trainmen still can be found today. But with grit and resourcefulness the logging railroaders accomplished the impossible regularly, and in not much more time than a similar feat might require today with modern equipment.

The logging trainmen, like the old-time woodhick, was a distinct breed from all others and made his own colorful contribution to the mosaic of mountain life in those earlier years.

TWELVE

THE GREAT DROUGHT OF 1930

In 1930, West Virginia suffered a drought of catastrophic proportions. In the memory of the oldest inhabitants of these hills, that drought was the granddaddy of them all. Like all droughts, it started out as a "dry spell," as we say in the mountains. It was not considered cause for alarm when it lasted a mite longer than usual, for over the years we had experienced many junior-sized droughts. Always they caused some discomfort, occasioned some crop damage, and dried up some of the poorer wells and springs. To such things we were accustomed, and it was all taken in stride.

As the dry spell persisted, it became more and more the topic of conversation and at church and elsewhere in casual meetings people were beginning to observe that it had been " a long dry spell." It became increasingly The Topic as the weaker springs went dry and the drilled wells without good underground supply began to fail and water shortage became an acute problem.

Ours was a religious community; and as the situation became more desperate, the more fortunate furnished water to relieve the distress of their dry neighbors, and virtually everybody was looking to God to take a hand in the matter. During the week they hauled water from the creeks to support their livestock; and on Sundays, as troubled, God-fearing people have done from time immemorial, they prayed for rain. As the situation worsened, a day of prayer was called at the church and the circuit riding minister was there to make the petition. The minister mustered one of his all-time efforts, which would have to go down in the religious annals as a masterpiece of extemporaneous prayer. Many of the congregation were convinced it was the most powerful plea they had ever heard. In fact, a few who lived on lower ground feared that he might have overdone it and opined that a prayer like that might bring down waters of such proportions that Noah's deluge would seem like a mini-flood by comparison. They made hasty plans to evacuate to higher ground, lest they be swept away. Unfortunately, however, the anticipated rain never came; a fact which the preacher attributed to the congregation's lack of faith.

By this time, cattle were really suffering and our parched crops were withering away. In desperation some of the farmers hired a young aviator to seed a cloud. He combed the skies for a cloud to seed, but finally abandoned the job, claiming he could not seed clouds which did not exist. Two area farmers gave a local man who professed to be able to remove warts with magic words five dollars to try to bring rain. Being an honorable wart remover, he cautioned his sponsors that he did not claim to be a rainmaker and, as it turned out, he wasn't. No rain.

By now people had begun to realize that they were experiencing the worst drought in living memory. Already they had seen the adversities that usually attended normal droughts. But now wells that had afforded water under every previous circumstance went bone dry, and springs that had never been known to fail before failed at last. As the smaller streams ceased to flow, farmers took recourse to the larger streams and creeks to relieve their stock; those who had the capital to purchase did not have the water and so the farmer was stuck. Finally the larger streams began to fail also.

What a sight it was to see vigorous streams that we had taken for granted gradually evaporate before our very eyes! If ever there were a symbol of perpetuity in the midst of so much mortality and transience, it would be our rivers and large streams, which certainly were here long before us and we expect them to be here long after us, eternally flowing on and on as they wind their way to some distant sea, incessantly renewing their strength with refreshing rains and winter snows. But alas, the rains failed and the drought continued until not one, but in our vicinity a half a hundred, strong streams that no one ever dreamed would lack a fish and a fisherman temporarily perished. It was quite depressing, and somewhat terrifying. Few things I ever experienced have served so well to revive a sense of man's dependence on his Creator and to awaken a renewed appreciation for the bounties of nature which we generally take for granted.

Of course there were a few deep wells fed by good underground springs which were not exhausted, as well as several sulphur springs which did not go dry. And those fortunate few who were blessed with a little water at the peak of the drought shared unselfishly with their waterless neighbors. In this way, people were able to survive; but most of their livestock was not so fortunate. Like all droughts, this disastrous dry spell eventually was terminated with belated, but welcome rain which once again revived our precious streams.

Like all nature's aberrations, this drought had some curious side effects and even an occasional amusing feature.

In certain areas in those days the manufacture of moonshine was a way of life. Besides the "shiner" (or operator) and a still, there were two essentials for the manufacture of this native product—water and corn. The drought exhausted the supply of both ingredients and brought this industry to an abrupt halt—something the law had never been able to do. As moonshine was considered by many to be essential to courting and fighting, romance and violence declined spectacularly during this long dry spell.

Being so scarce and the labor transporting sufficient amounts to get along being what it was, people were suddenly more frugal with water than money and found ingenious ways to make it go as far as possible. Jethro Hellems, telling how his wife conserved her supply, sometimes seemed to feel sorrier for the water than his wife. As he explained:

"Martha first uses the water to cook the meal and then after that, she uses it to wash dishes and then she will mop the floor with it. I swear she just wears that water plumb out. It don't have a bit of strength left in it when she gets through."

One of the disastrous side effects of the drought was the havoc it wrought with my uncle Saul's social standing. Up to a certain point in his generally undistinguished career, Uncle Saul seemed a born loser. He had a large familiy and a farm, when one day he inherited a little money and decided to leave the farm to homestead in the West. With his usual bad luck or poor judgment, he homesteaded poor and unproductive land with no salable appeal. Finally, he had to abandon it and return with his family to his poor mountain farm. As he was, he was no ball of fire as a farmer; he was able to eke out only a mediocre living. The only alternative was moonshining, but the shiners were efficient specialists and Uncle Saul being unable to compete with their talent seemed doomed to a life of penury and mediocrity when he developed arthritis. Now this was no ordinary arthritis. His particular kind was the type that enables its victim to forecast the weather more accurately than any known combination of meterologists and man-made weather instruments.

This weather-sensitive arthritis dramatically reversed Uncle Saul's declining fortunes and soon his fame as an unerring weather prophet made him a legend in our hills. Rare was the man who would attempt to mow his hay or go picnicking without consulting him. He was a man of distinction and standing in the community when the drought of 1930 set in. For some baffling reason, Uncle Saul's arthritis was cured with the advent of the drought, and with it went his reputation as a weather forecaster and his social standing. To his dying day, Uncle Saul bitterly resented the drought for curing his arthritis.

In those days, our mountain people knew nothing of Dow Jones averages or the Wall Street stock market. A while back a city slicker went hunting in the hills where he got in a discussion with an old veteran of the Great Drought on whose land he was hunting. In the conversation he mentioned losing much money in the stock market in 1929 and the Hoover Depression that followed. When the city man had gone, the old hillbilly turned to his wife and said:

"Ma, that feller' was lyin'. The stock market broke in 1930. You remember we had to sell them two steers for five dollars apiece 'cause there warn't any water or pasture and that caused the market to break. That's when that depression happened, too, 'cause all the stills had to shut down for lack of corn and water. That's one rap them fellers can't lay on old Hoover."

So don't waste time telling them old-time hillbillies that the stock market broke in 1929. The only one he knows about broke in 1930, when a good steer sold for five dollars if a man was lucky enough to find a man with five dollars and a water source.

THIRTEEN

THE STATE'S LAST LYNCHING

In the West Virginia coal fields it was traditional and sometimes necessary in mining towns to have some supplementary law enforcement to backstop the County Sheriff's Office. As West Virginia became the heart of the bituminous coal industry, mining towns were blossoming all over. The County Sheriff's office usually was understaffed and its tax collection duties spread its personnel too thin to enforce the law effectively. It was customary for the mining companies to recommend to the authorities some person to keep law and order in these places.

Naturally this practice gave rise to the common charge that these auxiliary peace officers were there to serve the will and bidding of the coal operators. In some cases this was undoubtedly true and gave the coal magnates a handy weapon at convenient times. On the other hand, many of these officers were good, honest men and a valuable adjunct to the Sheriff's office in maintaining law and order in the rough and tumble mining towns.

One such lawman was Joe Myles. Perhaps I am biased, for Joe was a personal friend and I had watched him in action for several years. Both the State Police and the Sheriff's office were shorthanded, so Joe was peace officer for five rib-busting, head-cracking mining communities in Greenbrier County: Bellburn, Leslie, Crichton, Quinwood, and Marfrance. These towns had sprung out of the laurel thickets almost overnight. They were boomtowns where men worked hard, played hard, and fought hard; and it took a man with a certain balance of temperament to enforce the peace and not bully. This it always seemed to me Joe Myles did admirably. He was firm, but not arrogant; genial, but not weak; knew when to crack down and when to ignore. Naturally he had his critics, some of them sincere, but I personally felt his judgment in enforcing the law without throwing his weight around was excellent. It always seemed to me he treated everyone with fairness and respect without any trace of prejudice or discrimination, a remarkable virtue in the 1930's when racial bias was much more common in

West Virginia than it is today.

For these reasons I am yet unable to comprehend why Joe was killed. I was not in the community when the following events happened, but I will give them as they were related to me for whatever historical value they might have. I do believe this account is substantially if not entirely correct. As to the guilt or innocence of the parties involved, I am not in position to pass judgment.

One evening in October, 1931, Joe Myles was called to come to Leslie from his Quinwood headquarters two miles away to put down a disturbance at a Negro dance. Joe and a young man named Brown who sometimes drove his car went down to the scene and, according to the story, explained to the dancers that their racket was disturbing the whole neighborhood. He asked them to have a good time, but to hold it down and warned that he would check a little later to make sure they were keeping it orderly.

As he promised, he returned and his arrival was greeted by a murderous blast of shotgun fire that killed both he and Brown. The State Police at Rainelle were summoned and rushed immediately to the scene where the bodies of Myles and Brown were surrounded by a throng of curious spectators. In the ensuing investigation information came forward that the shots were fired by two Negroes named Jackson and Banks. Shortly afterward they were arrested and jailed in Lewisburg, the county seat.

In the Negro community of Leslie everyone immediately clammed up. Suddenly no one knew anything damning about the shooting. Whoever had pointed the finger the night before now would not admit any knowledge of the facts in light of day. Try as they may, the police were unable to pin anyone down who had told them anything, for everyone insisted he said nothing, saw nothing, knew nothing.

Meanwhile it was the considered opinion of the community that the guilty parties were under lock and key. But obtaining a conviction seemed an unlikely prospect as the Negro Community was habitually uncooperative with the law in such incidents. Whenever in the past there had been cuttings and shootings in the Negro community witnesses managed to make themselves scarce or else assailants would plead self-defense and be convicted only of a deadly weapons charge when no one would testify to the contrary.

The Negro attitude, of course, was understandable. To

testify against another Negro in a white man's court was to him tantamount to turning on his own race. I feel the Negroes' suspicion of Greenbrier County justice was unjustified where the courts were concerned; but every instinct of the Negro, stemming from many ancient wrongs, caused them to protect their own under such circumstances.

As public opinion grew that a legal conviction of the alleged murderers could not be obtained, certain friends of the slain Myles determined that the parties they judged to be guilty must not get away with this cold-blooded killing and they hatched a plan to see that justice was done.

According to the plan, the lynching would be carried out sometime in deer season when most of the law officers would be in the woods. The organizers reasoned that with so many prominent citizens convinced that lynching was the only vehicle of justice, they could afford the risk of participation. There was the danger of someone talking when so many were privy to the act, but in case they were caught the more involved the more difficult legal reprisal would be. The conspirators agreed to meet at the foot of Brushy Run Mountain, some ten miles west of the Lewisburg jail, to finalize the plan. From there they would proceed enmasse to Lewisburg to snatch the prisoners for the lynching.

Approximately two months after the killing with deer season commencing and the law officers in the woods, the conspirators set their plan in motion. My information is that some fifty people met on the west side of Bushy Run Mountain just off Route 60 from whence they proceeded to the county jail in Lewisburg. When the jailer came to the door, the party ordered him to hand over Jackson and Banks. It was quite plain to the surprised jailer that the men meant business and were in position to enforce their demands, so he delivered the prisoners without resistance. I do not know whether the jailer was somehow immobilized or warned not to sound an alarm, but with virtually all lawmen out of town, he was probably helpless to avert the deed whatever he did.

Jackson and Banks were hustled westward on Route 60 by the lynchers and were hanged almost on the highway and shot to strings. Today tourists stop and visit the site where West Virginia's last and probably ugliest lynching occurred.

News of the lynching was splashed in headlines across the country. The publicity which ensued gave West Virginia the image of a lawless state inhabited by lynch-happy people running around with hangman's ropes looking for likely victims and convenient trees. This impression gained currency around the country in spite of the fact that there have been less than fifty such incidents in the entire history of the state.

Governor Conley naturally was upset over the bad publicity and immediately ordered a veritable army of State Police to descend on Greenbrier County and run down the perpetrators of this act.

The State Police came in swarms. They launched their investigation in Lewisburg with the jailer who told them a large number was involved. Later as some officers were driving along Route 60 they observed three men working on a broken down car. For some unexplained reason they stopped and in questioning the men became suspicious and undertook to search the car whereupon they found some guns. The men claimed to be deer hunters, but their story did not ring true to the officers, so they were taken in on suspicion.

It was alleged that the three men were taken to a Beckley, W.Va., hotel where they were grilled continuously for thirty hours, even stripped down, and walked with a trooper supporting them under each arm until they broke down and confessed what they knew. I cannot vouch for the accuracy of the report, but later events tended to confirm it. Supposedly the three men detained named every individual who started on the venture with the exception of a masked leader whom they could not identify. The force of their evidence was weakened legally by the fact that their car had broken down before they reached Lewisburg and the men had not witnessed the actual lynching. It did, however, give the police a lot of leads to work with in apprehending the individuals they felt morally certain to be guilty.

Proceeding on the information obtained from the other three men, the police next detained for questioning a young man of a prominent and influential family in the area. He was taken to a Rainelle, W.Va., hotel for quizzing, but before they could get to work on him he shrewdly placed his arm against a hot steam radiator, giving himself an ugly burn and the police an embarrassing situation. He then forewarned them that if they tried to put the heat on and break him down, that he would yell police brutally from here to kingdom come and any confession he might make would be worthless. He further threatened that his father would see that they were prosecuted for the same. Apparently intimidated by this approach, the officers released him and picked up a hopefully less wily man. They kept him on the griddle so long that he came back looking like a fugitive from Hell with singed-looking hair, bloodshot eyes, and a generally dishevelled appearance. It was rumored that he had been grilled extensively under a strong light close enough to singe his hair and leave him virtually blind temporarily.

Whatever the truth actually was, the local citizenry fully believed these rumors. In fact, some people who condemned the lynching were even more outraged by the alleged abuses of the investigating officers.

Undeterred by such criticism and armed with the information obtained from the persons they had taken into custody, the State Police decided to present the names of those involved with the exception of the unidentified masked leader to a Justice of the Peace court for binding over to the Grand Jury. When the day arrived for the police to present their evidence, they were met at the Justice of the Peace office by a huge crowd of indignant and, in some cases, prominent citizens whose presence seemed to congeal public opinion that the State Police actions were fully as reprehensible and perhaps more preveable than those of the lynchers.

Sensing the passion of public sentiment against them, the story goes that the police hastily caucused with the three men first arrested and privately made a deal: that if they would not bring charges against the officers, the police would not offer enough evidence to have them bound over to the circuit court.

Whatever happened, no one was ever tried for the lynching. In time ill-will over their investigative tactics abated, but I understand that yet today the State Police do not enter the premises of this man.

It could be that some of this story is pure fantasy, but it is the record of what is believed in that area about what was to my knowledge West Virginia's last lynching.

Note: As a direct result of my brother's account of this lynching, I have learned from a very reliable source some additional facts about this lynching which my brother may not have known.

My informant knows the men involved and confirms that this man, whatever one may think of police tactics, was indeed one of the lynchers.

Perhaps the most interesting footnote to this account is that the "unidentified masked leader" has been identified. He has been in the past a ranking law officer in a county municipality and is described as having "the perverted courage and callousness" to do such a thing. This man admitted his role one time to my informant while drinking together.

I have learned also that one relative of ours hid in our place in the country for two days because he was afraid he would be forced to transport some of the lynchers to the scene. He is not listed in *Profiles of Courage*.

FOURTEEN

AN EPISODE IN THE HATFIELD-McCOY FEUD

The Hatfield-McCoy feud is acknowledged to be one of the great feuds in American history. Most people have heard of it and know that most of the events related to it transpired within the borders of West Virginia. Beyond that this generation has little knowledge of its history.

One of the more interesting happenings involved a famous railroad detective by the name of "Iron" Dan Cunningham. Cunningham himself related this episode; and, if I recall correctly, I read the account in a Sunday edition of the Charleston Gazette sometime in the 1920's. I am depending upon recall for this incident, but I know that it is substantially what Iron Dan reported.

This event occurred when the feud was receiving its greatest publicity. The then Governor was disturbed about the bad image the affair was creating for the state. So he called in this famous rail detective and asked him to use his ingenuity and work his way inside where the feud was going on and find out the facts of the case, what the feud was all about, and report back to him. Iron Dan was given complete liberty to work at his own discretion.

I do not recall the name Iron Dan used in trying to infiltrate this battle ground, but you can be sure it wasn't Cunningham. We will say it was "Sullivan." In any case, he posed as a Bible salesman, because it was a nice, innocent occupation and also a rather common one in these times. Outfitted with a portfolio of order blanks, sample Bibles, and other items a real Bible salesman should have, he headed off to con his way into the Hatfield inner sanctum. Finally late one evening he managed to arrive unscathed at the home of Devil Anse Hatfield, the notorious old he-coon of the Hatfield clan. He introduced himself as "Mr. Sullivan," a Bible salesman. Devil Anse cordially invited him to supper and he was shown the lavish hospitality for which Devil Anse was noted if entertaining a friend. If I recall, a couple of Devil Anse's sons or kinsmen were also present. After supper they chatted and then at bedtime, Devil Anse got out the family Bible, read of the Book, and then had prayer, according to his custom.

So far, so good, thought "Sullivan." About that time Davil Anse turned to "Mr. Sullivan," who was still mentally congratulating himself on his cleverness, and said, pointing to a ladder leading to the upper story of the house:

"*Mr. Cunningham*, you may sleep upstairs. You will be allright up there. Just stay until we call you."

The mention of his real name with Devil Anse's instructions chilled Iron Dan's blood. That night he died a thousand horrible deaths, not sleeping a wink and perspiring all night wondering by what cruel means he would die the next day and if anyone would ever learn of his passing.

The next morning Devil Anse called for him to come down. He was given a hearty breakfast, but his appetite was not of the highest order, since he felt this was undoubtedly part of the Hatfield ritual before an execution. He frankly could not see much future in this particular meal. After breakfast Devil Anse, reaching for a cow bell with a leather strap attached, addressed Iron Dan:

"Mr. Cunningham, don't worry. You will be safe as long as this bell doesn't stop ringing within Logan County."

With that he put the cow bell around Iron Dan's neck. Feeling he had a new lease on life, Cunningham headed with his bell ringing for the nearest route out of Logan County, haunted every step by the suspicion that he was being watched by unseen eyes. He said he had no idea where the boundaries of Logan County were located, but he would darn well bet he was at least ten miles beyond them before he let that bell quit ringing.

At last account, so far as the great rail detective knew, the governor still had no first hand report on the feud, but Iron Dan was dead sure he personally had sold his last Bible in an effort to get one. If the Governor was still curious, he would have to get a new boy.

FIFTEEN

THE SKUNK HILL AFFAIR

Some of our hillbilly rowdies were so tough they didn't know trouble when it happened. One such roughneck was a local woodhick called "Lefty" Boley who was about as tough as the jawbone of a large ass.

Probably the most amusing example of his wonderful naivete along this line occurred one night at Skunk Hill, a notorious trouble spot.

The story was related by our country constable. As he told it, he received a call one night from Ethel Fenwick at Skunk Hill. Said Ethel:

"I wish you would cum down here. There's bin a little trouble."

Past experience having removed all doubt where Skunk Hill was concerned, the constable hastily hung up, grabbed his gun and billy, and lit out for our mountain version of Hell's Kitchen.

When he arrived at Ethel's cabin, it looked like it had been stampeded by a herd of cattle. The windows were broken out, the stoves overturned, and the bed looked as if it had been trampled by an elephant. The scene was one of chaos and ruin.

When Constable Jones inquired what happened, Ethel explained:

"Lefty Boley an' anuther feller wuz here visitin' me and my sister, an' some other fellers cum along and decided to run 'em off. Now I'm not goin' to git mixed up in court by bringin' any charges, but I wish you could see iffen somebody would make up to me fer all this damage."

The constable then set out to find Boley whereupon he summoned him to appear before Squire McClung, the justice of the peace. At the hearing the Skunk Hill sisters refused to press charges against Lefty because he hadn't started the ruckus and steadfastly insisted they didn't know the others. The Squire then asked Lefty the identification of the other parties involved. Boley swore he knew nothing about any trouble. Getting a trifle impatient with all this, the Squire leveled a finger at Boley and demanded:

"Lefty I want to know—and I mean right now—who that feller is who was with you at Ethel's place and how all this trouble got started."

Lefty was really an amiable character who merely had the curious habit of meeting trouble at least half way and coming out on top. Trying to cooperate, Lefty gave the magistrate this account of the episode:

"Squire, I don't know who that feller wuz. All I know is that I wuz settin' on this stump drinkin' a little moonshine and tendin' to my own business when this here feller cum along and asked if I knew where we could find some girls and I said we could do down to Skunk Hill and see Ethel Fenwick and her sister. He said, 'Well, let's git goin',' and so we set out. We wuz jist settin' there in the cabin an' this here car drove up with three fellers in it. One uf 'em run up to me and said, 'Hey, you clod, you cain't horn in on my girl thataway. I'm goin' to run you offa here.' I said, 'You and who else?!' Then that son-uf-a-gun made a pass at me with a knife and sliced a sliver offa my chin. One of the girls hit him over the head with a bed slat. Then one of them other fellers run in and shot out the lamp and the third one run in an' grabbed this here feller with me and flung him through a winder. Then somebody grabbed another bed slat and hit one of the girls with it and about that time I heerd one of the stoves git turned over. Things started gittin' a mite out of hand and looked like it might git personal after while. I wuz gittin' afraid somebody might start somethun', so I fetched my hat and went home. Effen there wuz any trouble, Squire, it wuz after I went home."

The Squire and Constable Jones conferred briefly and decided to drop the whole matter since all the trouble obviously had been a fantasy of overly-impressionable minds.

76

SIXTEEN

THE FIRST RAMP CLUB

One of the best storytellers and conversationalists I have ever known was Dr. Jim McClung, founder and owner of McClung's Hospital in Richwood. A handsome man with a shock of white hair and a vast fund of fascinating stories, Dr. McClung had a rare talent for tailoring his stories to the situation. He also had the distinction of being the charter president of what was believed to be the first ramp club in existence. At present there are a number of them, but as far as I know, Dr. McClung originated the first one.

Probably there are many readers who have no idea what a 'ramp' is since it is a mountain plant and not generally known to lowlanders. I have been told that it is indigenous to the Appalachian highlands and is not to be found elsewhere. There are two schools of thought as to just what a ramp is. To many it is a small, wild plant growing in the wood imbued with the blended fragrance of a strong onion, a frightened skunk, and a dead horse and utterly unfit for human comsumption. To another class of gourmets it is a delicate herb more toothsome than the manna of heaven and the living end of the perpetual search for the Fountain of Youth. Ramp fanatics sometimes opine that Ponce de Leon would be alive today and enjoying the vigor of youth if he had quit messing around in Florida hunting for a silly spring and had eased up into the West Virginia hills for a mess of ramps.

Whichever school of thought one prefers to believe, it does seem that the ramp is a cousin of the onion family and all initiates would agree that their odor is so strong that eating them assures privacy if one is the hermit type.

Richwood is the heart of the ramp country and because ramps were so popular with many people and because it also offered the distinction of belonging to the only club of its kind, a great number of people joined the Richwood ramp club. In due time its fame spread and many outsiders were initiated into the club. Because it was such a good place to get exposure to people who cast votes, it was inevitable the political figures soon began to join.

On one memorable occasion Governor 'Rocky' Holt came from Charleston accompanied by the popular and well-known Arthur Koontz, then the state Democratic national committeeman. Both men had applied for membership in the club and just to make it appear that they were a most exclusive and discriminating institution, the application of Governor Holt was jestfully rejected and Koontz was accepted.

Arthur, who had never eaten a ramp, asked the President:

"Dr. McClung, is a ramp really as strong as people claim?"

"Well, Arthur," replied Dr. McClung, "you will know after your initiation, but meanwhile I will tell you a story that may satisfy your curiosity.

There was once a mountain boy whom for the story's sake we will call 'George.' George emigrated to a distant city in another state where by hard work and application to duty he became quite successful. One day in his office with vacation time rolling around, his thoughts turned to his boyhood home in the West Virginia hills. Homesick for the hills, he shortly thereafter returned to West Virginia for a nostalgic visit. He finally arrived in the little village where he had grown up and took off on a winding dirt road to a little place about a mile out where his only living relatives resided—his Aunt Mary, his deceased mother's sister, and her husband, Uncle Jim and their son whom everyone called "Little Jim."

It was Sunday and as he drove up in front of the house there sat Aunt Mary dressed in her Sunday best waiting to go to church.

George emerged from his car and greeted his relative:

"Hello, Aunt Mary. How are you? You look as well as you ever did.

"Well, howdy, George," she responded, "You sure look well and prosperous."

"Thank you," said George, "how are Uncle Jim and Little Jim?"

"Oh, they're well," assured Aunt Mary, adding: "Little Jim's even bigger than Big Jim. Fact is, we're havin' sort of a problem with that boy."

"What's the trouble?" George inquired.

"Well, it's a mite embarrassing, but the plain truth is, we can't break that youngun' from suckin'. He just insists on doin' it right in church, even when the preacher is preachin'. We don't know what to do. The neighbors sit there and kinda sniggle 'cause most of them broke their children by the time they was in the eight grade.''

George was mortified at such a thing and determined a solution couldn't wait another Sunday.

"Aunt Mary," he exclaimed, "this has to stop. Who ever heard of a thing like that!"

With that he jumped in his car and took off for the village from which he returned shortly with a drug store remedy. He handed it to his aunt and instructed:

"Here is some epicac, Aunt Mary. Get out there in the outhouse and smear each breast generously with it and I'll guarantee you he won't suck again."

Aunt Mary followed his instructions carefully and had returned when Uncle Jim and Little Jim came out and greeted George. They all loaded up and went to church. Sure enough during the service while the preacher was reading from the Book, Little Jim wanted his maternal pacifier. His mother tried desperately to shussh him, but he wouldn't be denied. She finally relented and he commenced his embarrassing ritual.

Suddenly he gasped and fell over in the floor in what looked like an epileptic seizure. Some of the men grabbed him and rushed him outside where they began to fan him as he gasped for air. When he finally regained his breath, his first indignant words were:

"Pa, Ma's been eatin' them durn ramps again!"

SEVENTEEN

BUCK THE BAD

An old adage popularized by mountain preachers contends that there is a little good in the worst of us which needs only to be uncovered and cultivated. But there was a mountain character named Buck whose behavior sorely challenged this theory, if it did not refute it altogether. If godlessness is goodlessness, Buck was of all men most godless.

I first heard of Buck when I was about 12 and he, I suppose, was perhaps 19. On that occasion Buck had just enhanced his reputation by loosening the brake lock on a heavily loaded wagon parked on a hilltop, causing the wagon to plunge over the hill, demolishing wagon and all. In twenty years of my acquaintance, no one to my knowledge every knew of Buck performing a single act of benevolence, not even unwittingly. This was especially hard in the mountains where the good neighbor policy was a way of life, each man recognizing that all lived better and longer by that doctrine. Buck, however, was a glaring exception. In vice he was a thorough individualist and went about his misdeeds with almost amoral detachment.

Quite understandably, Buck was not exactly coveted by respectable parents of the community as a proper squire for their young ladies. The girls, however, were not always so particular or discerning and often turned up with Buck as their escort, much to the chagrin of their frantic parents who invariably took steps to terminate the relationship. To all such hubbub, Buck was sublimely indifferent.

One of the more serious incidents of this nature occurred one night at our church. A stepfather who had forbidden his stepdaughter first to go with Buck proceeded to grapple with Buck who decked him unceremoniously. The church elders and some other members decided to step in, lining up solidly against Buck and romance. Seeing he was outnumbered about eleven to one, Buck equalized the situation by pulling an old owl-head revolver whereupon he attempted to ventilate the Sunday School superintendent. Grabbing at the gun in desperation, the pistol hammer almost amputated the superintendent's thumb as Buck pulled the trigger. At this point the bystanders overpowered Buck and turned him over to the constable who with the superintendent hustled him to jail in Summersville where he was to be charged with disturbing public worship, carrying a deadly weapon, and assault with intent to kill. Buck never arrived. About five miles out of Summersville, Buck told his captors that nature was calling and requested permission to relieve himself. Seeing no hazard in this since Buck was handcuffed, they granted his request. A moment later he hurdled a high bank and, being the more agile of the three, eluded his surprised pursuers, jumped aboard a Pardee and Curtin log train and managed to get home ahead of them, pack up, and escape to Georgia.

After several months in Georgia, Buck, like every displaced mountaineer, got homesick and wanted to return to West Virginia. He began negotiating for favorable terms through a member of the County Court who was a friend of the family. It was finally agreed that if Buck returned voluntarily, he would stand trial only for carrying a gun under the so-called Johnson Pistol law, which entailed a mandatory minimum sentence of six months. Buck came back and drew a six-month sentence.

Buck had no sooner been sentenced than he began laying down on his fall schedule to the sheriff. In those days it was still the custom to work prisoners. Buck, however, informed the cowed sheriff that he intended to do no labor during his term. Furthermore, he brazenly announced, he expected day liberty to stroll about town. He came dangerously close to thoughtfulness when he condescended sleep in a cell at night. To these outrageous demands, the sheriff yielded meekly and it was almost his undoing. Buck exploited his liberty to the fullest, soon striking up a romance with a local girl. Each day they got together at Fatty Groves Ice Cream Emporium for a soda. This went on until his term was nearly up and Buck showed up at the local high school at Parents' Day with his new flame. This was the straw that threatened to break the camel's back as the parents were furious. The sheriff's daughter hastened home after school and served notice to her father that if Buck wasn't locked up, he could chuck any idea of reelection, even as garbage collector. The sheriff then went to Buck, explaining that he only had three days to go on his sentence, and made an impassioned appeal for Buck to spend them in jail. Buck reluctantly consented, coming about as near to an act of charity as he ever did in his whole ornery career and he regretted it ever afterward.

Buck was in and out of trouble—mostly in. One day I ran into Frank Posten, a husky 210 pound state trooper, and he looked as if he had been run down by Cassius Clay. When I asked what happened, Frank explained that he had had an unpleasant encounter with bantam Buck, who weighed a mere 150 pounds. According to the trooper, he was attempting to run Buck in on a warrant for the possession of liquor, when Buck warned Frank he would have to do it the hard way. Frank decided that with the weight difference if he couldn't take Buck without using his billy, "he could just go free." As Frank described it, it almost came to that.

"I grabbed him," the big trooper related, "and he started swinging. We fought all the way down the club house stairs clear out in front of the company store. He darned near licked me, but he was finally outwinded by my weight."

Buck eventually pleaded guilty to the liquor charge which had led to the fiasco with Posten and was given 90 days in jail. Asking the judge to allow him a word, Buck explained that he had some potatoes to dig as well as other urgent personal matters and urged the judge to postpone the start of his sentence until October 1. Permission was graciously granted.

The day before he was to begin serving his time, Buck parked himself on a ten-gallon keg by a roadside at Orient Hill where he began hitch-hiking to the Greenbrier County jail. Trooper Posten happened along and stopped to chat with Buck for a few minutes. When Frank inquired where Buck was heading, Buck reminded the officer of the 90-day stretch which he was due to begin. Posten noticed the keg on which Buck was perched and became curious. Explained Buck without batting an eye:

"Oh, that's my liquor. I thought I might want an occasional drink and maybe peddle the rest for spending money while I'm doing my time." The trooper thought surely Buck was pulling his leg, but ever wary of his shinnanigans, he figured he'd better check. Sure enough, Buck had ten full gallons of moonshine in the keg. This earned Buck free transportation to Lewisburg where his fabulous record was embellished with a fresh charge. Buck was locked in one cell and his keg of moonshine in another.

When Buck was tried on the second charge, the jailer was ordered to bring in the confiscated moonshine as evidence. Moments later the red-faced jailer returned to the courtroom lugging an empty keg. Naturally, everyone suspected the jailer himself had put the contents to good use since he alone had the key to the cell where the moonshine was being stored. The jailer knew very well the circumstances tended to compromise his integrity and his countenance was fairly glistening with embarrassment when Buck, who never seemed to know when he was ahead, blurted out almost chasteningly:

"I brought this liquor here for my personal use, to drink and to sell. So the second day I was here I made me a key out of a spoon. I drank part of it and sold the balance."

The second charge was therefore thrown out for lack of evidence.

A few days before Buck's term was up, the jailer discovered him missing from his cell one night as he was making room for a new 'guest.' His inquiries about Buck's disappearance to the other prisoners were rebuffed with a wall of silence. Thinking it incredible that a man would break jail with only four or five days to go on his sentence, the jailer initiated a search of the entire jail. Finally, to his utter astonishment, he found ol' Buck comfortably bedded down with a female cellmate in the women's side of the jail. Gasping, the jailer screeched:

"Buck, what on earth are you doing over here?"

"Milt, I like it better over here because the prisoners are friendlier on this side. I just made me a key when I first came in and I've been sleeping over here every night."

This was undoubtedly true since there were no official night checks with all the prisoners being short-termers.

Between jail terms Buck kept himself occupied with a mischievous "revenuer and shiner" game at which he was pretty adept. Buck, pretending to be a revenuer, would conceal himself while a moonshiner made a run. About the time the moonshiner was ready to hide his precious 'dew,' Buck would yell:

"Rush 'em, boys!"

Then dropping a broad hint of the most likely exit for the shaken 'shiner, Buck would add quickly:

"Some of you fellows hurry and close that gap over to the next hill before they get away!"

It might have proved a trifle embarrassing for Buck if any of the many moonshiners upon whom he played this little hoax had stood their ground to fight. Apparently, however, they figured it was better to be safe than sorry and invariably they scampered frantically for "the gap." By this clever deception, Buck captured more moonshine than any legitimate officer in the area. He, of course, put it to more constructive use than the law would have—at least by his definition of the term.

While it would take a volume to chronicle all his fantastic forages, I trust this snapshot of Buck's virtueless career will help you to understand why he is such a memorable character.

If Buck had any good qualities, he zealously and manfully concealed them from prying eyes.

EIGHTEEN

THE LADY YOU ROOMED WITH

In former years when the dogwoods were blooming and the trout were rising and the ramps were temptingly tender, a few of our local businessmen would get the urge to take off for the Yew Pine mountains or the wilds of Cheat Mountain to fish a little, eat a few ramps, and leisurely survey the splendid grandeurs of that great land God created especially for hillbillies.

While the menfolk looked forward to this traditional week in the wilds with unmitigated joy, the women-folk often viewed it with suspicion and foreboding. Many of them wondered if this vacation was really the stag party it was trumped up to be. They envisioned their men actually lying around drinking, playing poker, and dallying with the mountain girls.

With the wives in this frame of mind, it was inevitable that embarrassing situations would arise. One such incident came about when a certain fishing party made camp far up in the wilds of Pocahontas County near their favorite fishing stream and ramp patch. The place where they stayed was run by an elderly lady who had comfortable beds and could prepare food fit for a hungry fisherman, being a cook of no mean renown.

Radio was just then coming into wide use and television, of course, was unheard of. And in out-of-the-way places even radio in those days wasn't too well known. One of the fishermen, being a hardware and appliance dealer and deeply appreciative of the hospitality of his widow hostess, offered her a terrific buy on a radio. He said he would let her have one at absolute cost because she had been so nice to his party. Whenever she wanted one, he asked her just to let him know and he would ship it by express to Durbin, W.Va., where she could have it picked up.

As fate would have it, the appliance dealer's wife was his secretary and worst still, one of the most suspicious and unenthusiastic wives about these annual stag-party vacations. She had long suspected her husband just might be a gay blade in his dangerous forties when the following letter arrived for her husband:

Dear Mr. Knight:

I am the lady you roomed with when you were fishing up here. If you remember, you promised me a radio at that time. You may send it now as promised to Durbin, W.Va.

Yours very truly,
Mary Walkup

Mrs. Knight went up in smoke and flames. When she found her innocent husband, she hysterically thrust the letter under his astonished nose and never did even Rip Van Winkle get a worse harangue than poor Mr. Knight.

In desperation he turned to his fishing buddies to support his story. But for them it was just too good to pass up, so they deliberately added fuel to the fire by defending Mr. Knight in such a flimsy way as to sink the knife even deeper.

Finally it got to the point where there was going to be either a divorce or no more mountain fishing trips. Mr. Knight was able at last to salvage the situation only by taking Mrs. Knight along to deliver the radio in person to the widow who was thirty-five years his senior.

Knight was never able to live the incident down. For years people would teasingly inquire if he had received any letters from the widow lately. He invariably responded to these jokers with an unprintable invitation for them to go to a place where the fish don't bite and the ramps can't grow.

NINETEEN

MY UNCLE

Since both my parents' people were prolific, I was blessed with a veritable tribe of uncles and aunts. As we used to say, "I come of a large family on both sides of the house."

One of my uncles was a particulary proud man with a certain philosophical bent and an inherent distrust of Washington bureaucracy. In the latter respect I suppose he was somewhat ahead of his time.

It was not uncommon to overhear my uncle as he plowed baring his agitated soul to his mule Bill, which was always a good listener. On one occasion I can recall him expounding to Bill the absurdity of the human situation in words to this effect:

"Bill, there you are, a mere mule, the son of a jackass and here am I, a man made in the image of God. Yet year after year we work together and we eat together. Of all the crops I raise, you consume one-third while I share the remainder with a wife and five children. For that you must only plow while I must also buy the supplies, seed the soil, and hoe and shock the grain. Of course, I get to vote and you don't, but don't forget I have to pay taxes and you don't. Besides, I'm not so sure you didn't vote, considering who we got. Anyway, when you die, it is finished, but when I die it is Hell. Now tell me, Bill, which of us is really the jackass?"

Incredible as it sounds, this charming little story used to circulate about my uncle, who had an almost religious attachment to his farm which had been in the family four generations. He was supposedly quite distressed when at one time he was about to lose it. He had a $500 mortgage on the place, which normally would not have presented much of a problem. However, the Depression came, causing the banks to close and money therefore became scarcer than hen's teeth. A receiver was sent in to liquidate the affairs of the local bank who informed by uncle he must pay up or lose the farm. My uncle turned to everyone he knew who might be of assistance, but in vain. In desperation he finally turned to a preacher in a nearby community where he attended services. The preacher advised my uncle to turn his problem over to the Lord.

87

He took this counsel seriously even if a little naively. He is said to have written a touching letter concerning his problem which he addressed to "God." In heart-rending prose, he told the Lord how this farm had been his birthplace as well as that of his parents and great-grandparents. His children had been born there, too. Even the family cemetery was located on the property on a high knoll overlooking the house. His past, his present, and his future were inextricably bound up with this old homestead which was about to be taken from him for the paltry sum of $500. He humbly entreated the Lord to save his farm somehow.

The Postal Department was at a loss about delivering the letter for insufficient address and other problems, so the urgent plea of my distraught uncle wound up in the postal graveyard in Washington instead of Heaven. Apparently, the Lord got the message anyway, for the letter so touched the clerks at the Dead Letter Office that they took up a collection and forwarded $300 to my uncle. A short time afterward when the preacher ran across my uncle, remembering his recent problem, he stopped to inquire:

"Brother, what was the outcome of the problem I advised you to take to the Lord awhile back?"

"Well, preacher," my uncle answered, "the Lord sent me the money all right, but them greedy rascals in Washington took $200 of it."

Of such the spirit of conservatism was born.

TWENTY

THE PASSING OF A HILLBILLY

In the old days when funeral homes were scarce, burials in country communities, especially in warm weather, had to be carried out with dispatch due to the lack of embalming. The grave sites were usually near the church, often in the churchyard itself. Nearly all the services were conducted in the church by a circuit riding preacher.

When someone died in the community, the news spread rapidly by word of mouth and, in some cases, by country telephone. On one occasion a certain neighbor expired who had a 17-year-old son not especially distinguished for his intelligence or good taste. After his father had passed away late one night, the boy waited until about four o'clock in the morning when be began to dash from place to place awakening all the neighbors with the news that "the old man kicked the bucket last night." That was a common mountain expression for death, but it was used mostly in a very impersonal way by folks not close to the family. This young fellow later married and raised a family, but he was always remembered until he turned in by his tasteless announcement of his father's death.

The country stores stocked everything from mule shoes to lace curtains, including burial supplies. When a certain man died one day back on Burdette's Creek, the widow sent her two sons to the country store in our community to purchase burial garments for their deceased father. They first inquired about shoes whereupon the merchant showed them a soft sole lowcut on the order of a carpet slipper which was customary for burial in those days. As they hesitated, he also showed them a conventional lace shoe. For a couple of minutes the brothers conferred privately with the serious mien of a security matter and then the eldest emerged with the shoe decision. "We better take the lace shoes," he announced, "cause they'll wear better." Apparently the boys were taking in consideration where their father was going. A little later when they got to the shirts, the brothers ordered size 15½ colored shirt, explaining that "Pa won't wear a white one."

Sometimes in the case of a death, burial would take place

without the benefit of a circuit riding preacher. In these situations the family would have to call on someone in the community to read a few comforting passages of Scripture and to say a few words. When possible, however, a bona fide minister was always called. If the deceased happened to be a prominent person, it was unthinkable that his funeral would not be attended by a regular preacher. But that sentiment was reversed in my community at the burial of a local notable on a hot July day. The service had been set for two o'clock, but the preacher had not arrived when the time came. The crowd waited patiently. He still had not shown up at two-thirty. The preacher's horse had gone lame and his continued absence on a sweltering day made it necessary to take emergency action. Several friends of the deceased man approached the local school teacher, explained the situation, and begged him to take over the services. He was the best educated man in the community and, if they could not honor their friend with the attendance of a man of God, at least they could show their respect by having the next best man offer his final tribute, they urged. The teacher pleaded inexperience in such matters, but pledged to do his best. He took the pulpit and read the customary Scriptures. Then in the finest ministerial tradition, he extended his arms like a practiced person and asked the congregation to bow their heads. Finally he offered this famous prayer which in our community afterward ranked second only to the Gettysburg Address:

"O Lord, our dear brother has departed from us. When he was here with us, he raised game roosters and he fought them; he bred fast horses and he run them; he made good corn liquor and he drunk it. Of such is the kingdon of heaven. Amen."

With those brief, but moving words he sat down. He had paid the departed the highest tribute a man of my community could be given. From that day on, his eloquence was published abroad and many folks secretly hoped they too might be the beneficiaries of a preacher's lame horse when their time came.

TWENTY-ONE

THE INDOMITABLE MR. IVYHILL

Not too far from my boyhood home in the hills lived an affable eccentric whom I shall call "Mr. Ivyhill" since his family is a little touchy about what they regarded as "his weird sense of humor." Being a thoroughbred hillbilly, I personally thought it was delightful.

Mr. Ivyhill was a man of considerable wealth and had been educated in the prestigious Ivy League. As an officer in World War I, he spoke fluent French, German, and Spanish and was widely used as an interpreter. His financial interests were distributed among the coal, oil, gas and lumber businesses. But for all his affluence and culture, Mr. Ivyhill was at heart still a hillbilly who loved nothing no much as a good joke on a city-slicker.

A typical example of his sense of humor occurred one day when he was visiting a restaurant in unfamiliar parts. As the waitress approached with a menu, Mr. Ivyhill explained:

"I just want a snack. What kind of pie do you have?"

"Apple, peach, coconut cream, chocolate, and lemon," answered the waitress rotely.

"I didn't quite get that. Would you repeat it, please," Mr. Ivyhill requested. Once again the waitress reviewed the menu.

"Is it fresh?" Mr. Ivyhill inquired painstakingly.

Dutifully the waitress assured her customer all pies were freshly baked that day.

"Do you have cold milk?" he asked.

With a touch of impatience she promised Mr. Ivyhill that the milk would be as cold as a pawnbroker's heart. With that Mr. Ivyhill ordered his snack.

"Bring me a hamburger and a cup of coffee, please."

You can be sure the coffee and the waitress came back piping hot.

Mr. Ivyhill had his real fun at the expense of New Yorkers whose culture was too limited to contend with the likes of this versatile hillbilly. When he wished to be, Mr. Ivyhill was a man of impeccable taste and could be the veritable image of aristocracy in rich evening clothes. Ordinarily, however, he was never so inclined when he went to New York City. Instead he would outfit himself in expensive-looking dark, corduroy trousers and a dark shirt with an ill-matching dress coat, a costly Stetson hat, and a pair of Chippewa Cutter shoes, the trademark of a lumberman.

In this grotesque masquerade Mr. Ivyhill would check into the Waldorf-Astoria or some other swank hotel. Since his eccentric but expensive clothing affected wealth, he had no trouble getting accommodations. In fact, these hotels catered to these people, who often turned out to be some of their best patrons and greatest spenders.

As he loved to spar with waiters and waitresses, he was at his fun-loving best in the fancy dining rooms of these highbrow hotels. Unfailingly he would stroll in arrayed in the most ungodly apparel imaginable. As he was seated, a French waiter, or more likely a waiter with an affected French accent, would approach his table with a menu reeking with exotic dishes gathered from every place under heaven. Back then French recipes were considered the ultimate in fashionable dining and it was vogue in better dining rooms not only to feature French dishes but also their French names on the menu. This helped impress the diner.

Mr. Ivyhill would scan the imposing menu in apparent confusion to the secret delight of his snobbish waiter as he looked down on his hick customer with silent superiority. Ostensibly giving up, Mr. Ivyhill would sigh:

"Waiter, I don't see anything here I want. Just bring me a platter of fricasseed ground-hog and side dishes of turnip greens, chitlins and some grits, and a pint of Joe Jack's Aged-In-The-Wood Moonshine of 1923. That was his best year."

With this startling order the waiter would become unglued and urgently summon the head waiter to help explain to this clod that such items were unavailable. At this point Mr. Ivyhill would smile tolerantly and surmise that good food was a rare find in the city. Then to the utter astonishment of his contemptuous waiters, he would order in flawless French their choice dishes and best vintage wines, eat it in the most proper dining traditions, and leave a generous tip.

One of Mr. Ivyhill's better pranks was pulled on a railroad company. In our area the Chesapeake and Ohio line was the chief railroad, although Baltimore and Ohio had a branch line there. The C&O main line came directly down New River and went through Charleston and Huntington and on to Cincinnati. They had put on a crack train called "The Sportsman" which stopped only at important places such as Charleston, Huntington, and White Sulphur Springs, where it picked up the Pullmen and private cars of its millionaire clientele. Places like Gauley Bridge, Thurmond, and Prince this prestigious train blithely ignored.

One day Mr. Ivyhill had occasion to board The Sportsman, but had no desire to make a long trip to cater to its snobbery. Being a thoroughly original man, this was no problem to him. He just wired the C&O headquarters a telegram in these words:

"Large party of 60 wishes to board The Sportsman at Meadow Creek, W.Va., next Thursday going to New York. Please confirm if train will stop."

He signed his real name. The stop was quickly confirmed and next Thursday The Sportsman ground to a reluctant halt at Meadow Creek right on schedule. As Mr. Ivyhill stepped aboard the lordly train, the conductor inquired indignantly:

"Where is the party of 60 that had this train stopped?"

"I am the party that had the train stopped," replied Mr. Ivyhill.

"But we had orders to pick up a large party of 60 here," insisted the conductor.

"That is correct. I wired the head office that message," Mr. Ivyhill reassured the conductor.

With that the irate conductor blew a fuse and warned his new passenger:

"I will have you arrested for giving us false information causing this great train to strain its tight schedule for one passenger at a jerkwater stop!"

Unruffled and with a dismantling air, Mr. Ivyhill informed the upstart conductor:

"Pardon me, sir, but I was very careful to give your headquarters precise information concerning this stop. I am 60 years of age and weigh 255 pounds and if that, sir, is not a "large party of 60," would you tell me what is."

Nonplussed beyond a faint oath, the subdued conductor walked away—another victim of the indomitable Mr. Ivyhill—and The Sportsman moved humbly out of Meadow Creek with his large party of 60.

TWENTY-TWO

A HEROIC SPIRIT OUT OF THE RUGGED PAST

Several years ago I emigrated to the Mid-Ohio Valley, an area bounded by Wheeling on the north and Parkersburg on the south. Nestled halfway between the two cities is the pretty little town of Sistersville, the home of former Governor Cecil Underwood and formerly one of the great oil and gas centers of the country. Residents boast that the town once had sixteen millionaires and thirty-eight saloons. Even today vestiges of the community's distinguished past remain in the shadow of several stately mansions with manicured lawns and well-groomed shubbery.

In this town lives a remarkable lady named Hattie Ullman. Sistersville has nothing in its historic past of which it can be more justly proud than this incredible citizen. She is the impress of the spirit which made America great. In this sad day of federal aid to farm your own land, to grow Christmas trees, to have illegitimate children, it is a refreshing experience to meet a person who embodies the spirit of self-sufficiency or, as we hillbillies put it, "hoeing your own row."

Miss Ullman has been hoeing her own row quite a while. A music teacher, she started teaching professionally at age 14 and today at 89 she is still active. It is true that she went to college in the interval, but in the summers she continued to teach. Compounding the incredibility of her story is the fact that she has survived a contest with yellow fever, and though she is a diabetic, she yet today does not take any medication for that condition. What is more, she has suffered in recent years several heart attacks of such severity that occupants of neighboring apartments have heard her fall to the floor in unconsciousness. At times these attacks have caused her to be hospitalized for thirty days or so with little hope of survival. As if that weren't enough, she has also required several lengthy hospitalizations in recent years with bouts of pneumonia. In spite of all these adversities, which would have killed many and broken the spirit of the rest, Miss Ullman has roared back with each release from the hospital to call her students and pick up as if there had been no interruption.

94

In this vicinity there are grandmothers who were taught by Miss Ullman as well as their children and grandchildren. For all I know there may be even great-grandmothers or great-grandchildren around who received instruction from her.

In these days when strong, healthy men yearn for retirement and spend their leisure time tabulating the benefits they might draw if they retired at 62, it is reassuring to meet someone who has worked much longer than these lazy characters have lived with no thought of retiring.

Miss Ullman feels as long as she is able, she has a job to do, that every man is responsible before God to contribute his part, to use his talent, not to bury it. And for that philosophy, she is today at 89 far younger than some who are retiring at 62.

Recently my wife and I were going to dine at Springer's Restaurant in Sistersville. We had heard that Miss Ullman was gravely ill and probably would not survive. Imagine how shocked we were to discover Miss Ullman seated pertly at one of the tables! Being very fond of her, we joined her. It was a cold February day and she had walked two blocks to the restaurant. We were having a nice chat when she glanced at her watch.

"Please excuse me," she said, "but I have a pupil coming down from New Martinsville and it is almost time for her lesson."

So today Miss Hattie goes on like the mighty Ohio on whose banks she resides with no thought of the past, but only planning for tomorrow. Her motto might aptly be, "The past is for the weak and old. The future is for the strong and bold."

TWENTY-THREE

MY MOUNTAIN FRIEND AND FELLOW-TRAVELER

This book would not be complete without a tribute to my hillbilly friend and fishing partner of the last twenty years.

I doubt that one could find a more congenial fishing companion or truer friend than this sterling fellow who like myself is a mountaineer of Greenbrier County vintage. Since I would hate to lose him, I will use only his nickname of 'Bus.'

In addition to his other virtues, Bus is also a good driver, an expert boat handler in both calm and rough waters, and without doubt the most fanatical shortcut hunter since Marco Polo. This propensity of his has led us to frontiers unmatched since the settlers crossed the Alleghenies.

One time, for example, we were fishing the head of the Tennessee Valley impoundments, Lake Watauga, having traveled the conventional route via Bluefield, W.Va., Abingdon, Va., and Mountain City, Tenn. When we were preparing to return home, Bus with that only too familiar gleam in his eye broke to me the distressing news that he had discovered a surefire shortcut which would save us miles of travel, offer better roads and prettier scenery. An inherent conservative, I offered the usual conservative objections only to suffer the usual conservative's fate—I was outvoted. Frankly, I have never understood how he won that election by a margin of 3 to 1 with only two registered voters. Anyway, I wish I could describe the way we came, But I couldn't see for the undergrowth. I can tell you that we traversed uncharted mountains, broke in unnamed roads, and passed through Confederate settlements which had not yet learned of Lee's surrender or the Emancipation Proclamation. Yet I feel the adventure was not wholly in vain since we were able to persuade one farmer to release his five slaves. After many other incredible experiences too bizarre to record, we finally managed to break through a gap in the mountains back into the Bluefield-Bristol highway and get on home.

This is just one of dozens of Bus's recommended shortcuts and, like the true explorer he is, he is today as enthusiastic about them as he was twenty years ago. Not one of them has ever panned out and we have traveled enough extra miles to take us around the world twice in that time. Bus, however, is still trying and with the good maps coming out today and with the help of God, I believe there is a slim chance that one day we just might break even on one of these Rand-McNally adventures.

Bus and I considered at one time collaborating on a book tentatively entitled, *One Thousand Lakes Where NOT To Fish*. We knew that we might be swamped with lawsuits by dock and marina interests, but we could have saved American fishermen untold millions of wasted dollars. We had been keeping a strict record of these inhospitable lakes and had agreed when we reached one thousand we would quit angling and write this book as a public service to other devoted followers of Isaac Walton. The idea was abruptly dropped when one day we wound up at Lake Okeechobee, Florida, the best of many good lakes in that state. Many sportswriters laud the St. Johns River as the finest bass waters in the world while others give the edge to Lake George. A few would contest for other favorite spots. When the temperature is right and the bass are in a good mood, I would concede that the fishing in any of these well-known places is as good as the best. But from long experience I can affirm that day in and day out the Hayfield Lake, as Okeechobee is called, is the most incredible bass fishing in America. It has the longest spawning season, the best cover, the best food, and above all, the most catchable fish anywhere. For this reason I suspect Bus and I will never author our book on places not to fish since we quit looking.

Enough about the virtues of our favorite fishing spot. Let me proceed with my tribute to my favorite fishing companion who is as close to me as any of my brothers and more precious than jewels or fine gold. Recently I was hospitalized with my first serious illness. Bus came to visit me bringing with him a fifty dollar fishing reel as a get-well gift. I doubt that I need to tell any fisherman that this cheered me more than any doctor and ran my pulse higher than my prettiest nurse, which tends to confirm the theory that fishermen are not as other people.

One of the most endearing of Bus's wealth of sterling qualities is his great modesty and humble spirit. So many fishing partners annoy their companions with incessant needling or bragging. Not Bus. Once, for example, we brought into the dock where we were staying a tremendous string of large bass, which prompted the bug-eyed dock-owner to exclaim:

"That's the prettiest catch I've seen here in two years. Where did you fellows get them?"

After showing him a place exactly five miles from the spot of the catch, the dockowner remarked to Bus:

"You boys always catch fish when you are down here. Is that fellow with you a good fisherman?"

Bus responded with typical modesty like all nature's noblemen, waiving a golden opportunity to assure all and sundry that he was the real fisherman of the party:

"Yes," Bus humbly replied, "my buddy is the best fisherman I have ever hooked up with. In fact, when he is having a good day, he will catch at least a third as many as I do."

Unlike many anglers, Bus is not given to boasting about his record catches. Sometimes people who have heard of his prowess in this sport, especially of his successes in Florida and around Okeechobee try to pump him about his experiences. A few years ago some friends in South Charleston were trying to pin him down on a very huge bass he had snared on our first trip as I told them it was a tremendous fish. One fellow wanted to know how much it weighed. Bus explained that we never carried scales or weighed our fish. Then he wanted to know how long it was. Bus pointed out that we didn't carry slide rules either. Finally he persisted that Bus hazard a guess on the weight of the fish. To this insistence Bus yielded but not without remarkable modesty to the end. Said he:

"Personally I do not fish for trophy catches, but for the sheer sport of fishing. However, if you are mathematically inclined, I think I can give you some facts which will enable you to arrive at the exact weight of the fish you are asking about.

When I brough the fish into dock, a city-slicker tourist standing by got real excited about the size of the catch and asked to take a picture of it. I consented since he had a Polaroid camera that would develop the picture in only ten seconds. Instead of ten seconds, however, it took exactly four minutes to develop the picture of this bass. He was so excited about the picture that he rushed the negative over to the little post office at Morehaven to send it to his fishing buddy in Illinois. The negative weighed fourteen ounces and took seventy cents postage. That should help you determine the weight of the fish."

Personally, if I had caught such a fish, I would have been

tempted to have embellished the truth a little, but Bus always adheres strictly to the facts.

It is my fond hope that I may recover to rejoin this amazing adventurer and angler on another of his never dull excursions into America's hinterlands.

TWENTY-FOUR

THE DEATH AND RESURRECTION OF AN ORGAN

Incredible things do happen in the mountains, but few of them any more bizarre than an experience of one of our neighbors.

It all began when Henry, a middle-age proprietor of a small, but thriving business, and a person of presumably superior health, suddenly began to "go down hill," losing an alarming amount of weight. Word spread that Henry was seriously ill and everyone naturally suspected cancer. Quite worried himself, Henry decided to enter Johns Hopkins Hospital in Baltimore for diagnosis. Having a large family with three children still in school, Henry persuaded his wife to remain with the youngsters while he was gone. With all braced for the worst, Henry departed by train for Baltimore.

Tests at the hospital indicated gall stones. Surgery revealed no malignancy and Henry was informed, to his great relief, that his worries were over. Henry, delirious with joy, celebrated the news by purchasing an organ for his music-loving family. The salesman whom he had summoned to his bedside promised to ship it immediately by express while Henry recuperated. The arrival of the organ would be a token of his condition which the family would know how to decipher and Henry left it at that.

Back home few people expected Henry to return from Johns Hopkins. So when the organ arrived from Baltimore in a casket-like box, the man at the local express office surmised that poor Henry hadn't survived. He immediately contacted the family minister and had him break the dreaded, but not unexpected news to the family.

Before he had left for Baltimore, Henry, anticipating his demise, had left instructions for his burial. He had requested that his casket not be opened, that he be buried on the family plot, and that he be put away with the utmost dispatch. The family wished to honor these last requests and so services were held almost immediately. The preacher gave Henry a royal eulogy and afterward the box which presumably contained his casket and remains was buried just as it had arrived.

The Friday following the Sunday rites, Henry's oldest boy still at home was watching two men and buggy hastening toward their home, when he gasped with ashen face:

"My god, Ma! It's Pa! Pa is coming up the road in a buggy."

In disbelief the "widow" darted out of the house to see for herself. In those days ghosts were still a live issue and it was little wonder that she promptly fainted. Henry and his livery driver managed to revive her in a few minutes whereupon, vacillating between joy and alarm, she inquired:

"Henry! Henry, whom did we bury?!" Totally unaware of his recent interment, Henry wanted to know what she was talking about. Having explained about the arrival of the "casket" from Baltimore and their faithful observance of his last requests, Henry blurted in dismay:

"Ye-e-e gad! You buried the organ!"

Henry explained about the organ and shortly thereafter the instrument was exhumed from its lonely plot in the family cemetery still composed and in fine condition. It brought music to Henry's family for years to come.

So far as I know, this is the only burial and resurrection of an organ on record.

TWENTY-FIVE

MOUNTAIN STORYTELLER

One of the great mountain storytellers was Charlie Perkins. He was evidently born with this talent, as he became well known even in his early years, as a proficient and entertaining teller of mountain tales. His homely wit, and dry humor was a delightful addition to any group, and in the mountains where good storytellers abounded, Charlie stood tallest of them all. It would be easy to spend a couple of chapters recounting some of his sagas, but it would not be fair to retell Charlie's stories, as no one could retell them without losing much in the telling, so I will content myself in giving credit to Charlie Perkins, by saying unhesitatingly that he made longer tracks than any of his contemporaries or competitors in this field. I will only give one little episode that happened to Charlie whom many of us called the Philosopher, and he did have a philosophy that allowed him to meet and enjoy any situation he faced.

Now Charlie was as homely a man as we had in those hills, and he was married to a beautiful and talented woman who was a school teacher. They had a son age thirteen and a daughter eleven. Charlie had one weakness and that was that only occasionally, perhaps once a year, he would imbibe a little too much of Jo Jack's special white lightning; and while a little of it just oiled Charlie up to the point of loosening his tongue, a little more changed him completely, and then he changed from Dr. Jekyll to Mr. Hyde. He was so well liked, and his wife so respected, that when he got this way and had a little fight or something of this nature, it was always overlooked. Charlie being of a naturally sunny disposition would be penitent, and thus the matter would end. But on this particular occasion of which I am going to tell, it was the 4th of July and a baseball game was being played in Charlie's hometown with a neighboring town, and since Charlie bowed to no man in patriotism to country and hometown in celebration thereof, he had slightly overloaded on Jo Jack's special. What made the situation particularly tricky was the fact that it was Jo Jack's fighting liquor instead of his courting brew. Consequently, Charlie grew progressively louder, louder, and finally downright quarrelsome. It finally got to the point that the chief of police remonstrated with him, whereupon Charlie grandly advised him to go fly a kite, or milk a cow, or concentrate on any little project that he wished so long as it in no way cramped Charlie's style; but that if he in any manner bothered him, Charlie would be compelled to kick his rear end up into the vicinity of his shoulder blades. Even the good-natured chief could not quite swallow these words, so he took Charlie by the arm with the intention of leading him away. So Charlie did approximately what he had told the chief he would do, and to add insult to injury, he took the chief's pistol away from him and threw it in the river. For some reason Charlie's action seemed to offend the chief, and he deputized three or four men to help him, and for the first time in his life, Charlie was jailed. The Fourth of July that year was on Saturday, and that evening Charlie's wife came into the mayor's office, and apologized for him, and asked the mayor if he would not turn Charlie loose as she did not wish to have it against his record that he had spent a night in jail.

The mayor was personally fond of both Charlie and his wife, but he suggested to her that they would not book Charlie, and consequently, it would not be on record; but he suggested to her that they keep him in overnight, and he would be so humiliated that he would never repeat the offense. She agreed that it was a good idea, and this was done. On Sunday morning Mrs. Perkins came over to the jail, and she naturally assumed that Charlie would be absolutely overcome with shame, so she had the jailer to let her in to see him and to let her take her penitent and erring spouse home.

To her horror when she got back into the bullpen of the jail, Charlie was in absolute glory. Not that he needed a captive audience for his stories but he had one, and they were living it up. He had them in stitches and rolling in the aisles or rather their cells, and good showman that he was, he was enjoying every moment of it. She was utterly disgusted, and after just a few words with Charlie she abruptly turned and left. After she had gone one of the women prisoners which were across the corridor from Charlie but who were a part of his audience, said, "Charlie, who was that beautiful woman?" He answered, "That was my wife." The woman prisoner said, "Charlie, how in the world did a woman as beautiful as that happen to marry a man as homely as you?" Charlie answered her by saying, "Love is somewhat like lightning. It's just as liable to strike an outhouse as it is a palace,'' and come to think of it that is perhaps as good a summation as I have ever heard.

The woman prisoner then said, "Charlie, do you have any children?" and for some reason, perhaps just to see why she was asking, Charlie answered "No." The woman said, "How long have you been married?" and Charlie answered, "fifteen years." The woman persisted, "If you have been married fifteen years and had no children, what is wrong?" Charlie answered, "Nuthin that I know of." The woman said, "Charlie, if you have been married fifteen years and have no children, there has to be something wrong with one of you." Charlie said, "Nope. Nuthin wrong with either of us that I know of." The woman asked, "Well, how do you explain being married fifteen years and no children?" Charlie said, "Well, I'll tell you. When I was courtin my wife I propositioned her, and she raised so much Hell, I've never mentioned the subject since."

TWENTY-SIX

THE MOUNTAIN MEDICINE MAN

Although not indigenous to the hills, another of the colorful institutions of mountain culture was the itinerant medicine man and his covered wagon plastered with garish advertisements. In the hills physicians were scarce and ailments, real and imagined, were legion. Consequently, the mountaineer leaned heavily on patent medicines in which he put a lot of stock and of which there was no mean supply.

For every ailment there was a patent 'remedy.' Occasionally someone 'discovered' an ambitious medicine which was touted as a panacea for several unpopular maladies. Every country store was well-stocked with conventional patent formulas. A favorite with the men folk was *Dr. Pierce's Golden Medical Discovery* while the women catered to *Lydia E. Pinkham's Compound*. I once heard one leathery old mountaineer who was unable to read claim that after using the *Pinkham's Compound* by mistake, he began to blush at shady jokes and took up knitting and crocheting. Learning of his mistake, he said he threw away the balance of the bottle, took a manful chew of homemade twist tobacco, and recovered his masculinity instantly.

The unconventional formulas of the traveling medicine man could not be found in the country store, as they were hand-mixed by these crafty forerunners of the modern pharmacist. The chief ingredients of his potent remedies were branch water, a litte moonshine or alcohol to give it authority and coloring. Invariably the infirm seemed to feel better after a couple of doses of this invigorating solution.

The medicine men were con artists of rare talent, but they were welcome in each community as they peddled their remedies, brought news from surrounding communities, and furnished entertainment that relieved the routine of rural life. Sometimes they had a magician or perhaps a fiddler and occasionally even an Indian who performed native dances. Of course, the medicine man himself was a skillful entertainer in his own right and he practically mesmerized his audience as he promoted his latest medicinal 'discovery' which possessed almost magical curative powers hitherto undreamed of.

One stood out above all the rest that frequented our community. He was a commanding figure better than six feet tall with a Buffalo Bill goatee who called himself "Dr. Delaware." He was always dressed in tall hat, a long black coat, and striped morning trousers and he wore them with considerable distinction. He was accompanied on his circuits by an Indian who opened the show with vigorous war dances. Then before offering his exciting remedies for sale, Dr. Delaware would entertain the crowd with magic tricks, pulling rabbits and other unlikely and unexpected objects out of his stove pipe hat. Finally, he would mount the seat of his wagon and make his pitch, of which the following example is typical.

"Ladies and gentlemen. Over a century ago my great-grandfather was captured by the Delaware Indians. They liked him and finally adopted him. He soon observed that there were no illnesses in this particular village. Later he learned the reason why. The great chief of this tribe, Running Deer, besides being a great warrior, was very intelligent and had compounded a formula from native herbs which had eliminated sickness among his people. As my great-grandfather was a favorite of the chief, he hoped to procure this sensational formula and bring it to his own people. He was able to obtain it only after marrying Bubbling Water, the daughter of the chief. He then managed to escape and it has been the privilege of my family to be the custodians of this great discovery ever since. I have devoted my life to refining and improving this formula for the benefit of mankind. The tropics, the frigid zone, in fact, the four corners of the earth have made their contributions to this fantastic medicine in rare herbs which I have added. As a result I offer to you a compound which will not only cure the simple maladies of the Indians, but one that will cure the more complicated and multiplied ailments of white men.

"Ladies and gentlemen, I am offering you here and now an opportunity to conquer sickness once and for all with *Dr.. Delaware's Boon To Mankind*. Yes, ladies and gentlemen, this potent formula will humble the most dreaded diseases known to man. Before its magical power the worst cases of heart trouble must fall. Cancer will never again show its ugly face. Arthritis and rheumatism will be only unpleasant memories. Crutches can be used for firewood. Chills, fevers, aches, and pain need no longer be endured. Pneumonia, typhoid, and yellow fever will forever disappear. Whatever your malady, ladies and gentlemen, this remedy will break its hold. If you have no ailment, take a bottle of *Dr. Delaware's Boon To Mankind* as a precaution against the invasion of suffering.

Step forward, ladies and gentlemen, first come, first served. One dollar a bottle. Just a moment! Just a moment! I wish to make clear that should I have omitted any ailment, or if there should arise now or later any malady unfamiliar, this magnificent formula will doubtless cure them also. Step right up, ladies and gentlemen. Dr. Delaware's Boon To Mankind, one dollar per bottle while the limited supply lasts.''

Dr. Delaware did a land office business and departed to the next village to repeat his slick performance. Along the way he stopped at a secluded spot in the woods beside a sparkling mountain brook where, with the aid of its clear water, a half a barrel of moonshine and a little coloring, he filled two gross of bottles with this ancient magical compound refined and improved over a dedicated lifetime with rare herbs garnered from the four corners of the earth.

CHAPTER TWENTY-SEVEN

EARLY DAYS AS I LIVED THEM

Mrs. Betty Deitz at age 75

Mrs. Deitz was born at Nutterville, Greenbrier County, W.Va., Dec. 30, 1879, daughter of Issac D. Nutter and Mary (Walker) Nutter. She died July 8, 1980.

She went to a one-room school then to normal schools and was a teacher before 1900. She taught schools periodically for more than fifty years, as well as having nine children, including the first, Granville A. Deitz.

She wrote and told hundreds of stories and poems including the following autobiography of her first twenty years of life as it was lived in the mountains, nearly one hundred years ago.

This finds me approaching one hundred years of age, so grateful for my eyesight and that I have never lost interest in a book or the events of the day.....Often I pass away the time by writing a poem, such as it is, or scribbling a story for the grandchildren. Just now I took a notion to write a story of life as we lived it a long time ago.

For several years our old log house had served as a schoolhouse and as the only church of our neighborhood. It was one large room, one huge fireplace, with logs called puncheons flattened and used for a floor. By the time I was old enough to remember, these puncheons, which had been split flat side up, had been scrubbed as white as paper. I recall they were sometimes covered with sand and left to wear down, leaving them whiter than ever and shining. By the time my mother had become a bride, another schoolhouse had been built and my grandfather, who owned the land on which the school had been built, gave it to my mother and father, and that is where three of us children were born. When the family began to grow, and a baby girl was born, father decided it was time for an addition to the one room. He, with the aid of neighbors, built an upper story which we called our loft. The stairway led up on the outside of the house, and ended on a little platform against the big chimney. Then there was a door right over the landing which led into the loft. It was cold up there, and we used the big schoolroom downstairs for living quarters and bedroom for the entire family all winter long, and until we built our new house. Father also added a long shed to the big room, and it served for kitchen and dining room. Then he added a porch built of flattened and split logs, and connected with the outdoors stairway. He built a nice pair of board steps to this porch, and here is where I sat so often, especially during the evening twilight or early dawn, just wondering, I think. I wondered about so many things! Where the little breezes came from that whispered in the tops of our tall maple trees. Thought perhaps the Old Man In The Moon was trying to talk! Then the many birds came along, swinging and calling to their mates!

Oh, there were so many things to wonder about back then, and so many nice sounds to listen to! The little brook in front of my steps gurgled and danced as it ran swiftly down the hill and landed with a splash in the old sunken barrel from which we got our drinking water. From there it put on new strength and flowed along to our spring house, but I did not know at that time that our babbling branch would, after a long, long time, mingle with so many big rivers and by and by be in the Gulf of Mexico.

One bird I especially liked was a cardinal, a big red fellow that perched on a branch near my window and I thought he said "You are sweet! You are sweet!" Then there was a little invisible bird that always frightened me. That was the whippoorwill.

We heard so many ghost stories and ill omens that I was in a state of worry when one of these little whippoorwills came around, for I had heard that if they called real nearby, it was a sure sign of death! So I sat on my old steps in the evening and wondered "Could my mother or Dad die?" However, try as I could, I could not keep those little pests from sitting on the windowsill near me or in the hop vines at the end of the porch, calling, calling, "Whippoorwill! Whippoorwill!" It lasted through the entire spring, and now they are almost extinct it seems, and we seldom hear their call. I really miss them. Perhaps it is only fancy, but it seems to me that everything was more intense in those far-away days! Storms were fiercer, cold more cold, so many butterflies and wild birds of every color and kind! Then we had wild animals that sometimes gave us a fright and sometimes a thrill. I remember when some neighbors came in and told of hearing the old panther scream like a woman, and sometimes we were afraid to go to the woods for berries. We children, with our cousins, often went across the creek for wintergreen (or tea) berries, and one day we found a big brown bear quietly eating berries nearby! Needless to say, we hurried out of the woods and left him to enjoy his dinner!

Also, we had many pet animals. I was seldom without a pet lamb that followed me about and came at my call. Then it was quite an event when Old Nell found us a little crooked-leg colt—almost as big an event as when our new little baby brother arrived! This was long before the days of the stork, so we children were much puzzled. My dad saved the day by telling us to look around old stumps as we walked through the snow to school and maybe we would find baby tracks. It was a long route to school that day, up and down hill looking in vain. All we found were small animal tracks, but later we thought for certain that we would get a new baby brother, for there were his tracks in the snow as clear as daylight! We later learned it was a coon track, so much like a baby's! We could often hear the howl of a mountain cat, but I never saw one. Very often I saw foxes, for there were so very many of them. They would get among our lambs and chickens. I remember so well the night Dad called me out of my snug bed to carry the lantern. Something was among the sheep! We did all right until a frightening screech threw me into a panic! I sent the lantern as far as I could and grabbed Daddy's leg! How he did laugh! It was only a little screech owl nearby. Do birds play pranks, I am asking?

There were many interesting days for us children, hard work days for our parents, but we enjoyed the special big dinners. The neighbor women who came to help often brought playmates for us. These are a few of such days: Logrolling Day, Goose-picking Day, Hogkilling Day, the Last Day of School, and last but not least, a few weeks of Revival Meetings when school was dismissed. We attended about three church services each day. The old log church rang with song and shouting! Logrolling Day came after long preparation when the summer work was done. Father had already planned a new piece of woodland to be cleared for corn planting next spring. No matter how large the trees, they had to be ringed so they would die and fall out by root, or they must be cut down and all the limbs cut off and the brush picked up and burned. This was a task in which the entire family could take part, but not altogether an easy job. Then all the logs had to be sawed into long sections and readied for the big Logrolling Day! The neighbor men came, their wives came, and some of our cousins came, so we children looked forward to that one day in early spring. Every woman pitched in to help prepare the big feed. Later, when the weather was just right, the moon in its full, the neighbors gathered again to burn off our clearing. How our cousins and we all enjoyed watching the big bright fires and the million sparks of light that floated sky-high almost to meet the stars overhead!

Hogkilling Day was rather interesting also, at least for us children. The hogs, fattened on the fallen chestnuts, were herded into a pen near the house. Early in the morning, father would start the day with an immense fire, logs piled high, and dozens of sand rocks placed on top. A large barrel was sunk part way into the ground and filled with water. Later, when all was ready, the big hot rocks were thrown into this water where the poor pig would be doused head-first as soon as his last squeal was heard. Then the scraping was started, for all the hair had to be scraped off as soon as the hot water loosened it,

111

and soon there was a neatly-sheared animal. How I did hate to hear the last squeal of our pet pigs! Then came the dressing, the cutting into pieces, rendering of lard, and the sweet taste of new pork! But we were usually ill by the end of the week, for the taste of fresh pork was too much to resist. There was no fresh meat on the market back in that day, so it was chicken always, or a lamb once in the summertime.

Goosepicking Day was rather interesting too. It came in the early summer, so the poor geese when naked wouldn't freeze. Of course, when Goosepicking Day came, we always called on my handy aunt who we said knew how to do everything, Aunt Catherine! We herded the geese into a shed, and my aunt, seated on a solid chair, would grab a goose, throw it across her lap, and my, how the feathers would fly! Along with every handful of feathers would come a shrill quack from the old bird she was treating so cruelly! Geese are very interesting fowls. The males, ganders, make devoted husbands, the old folks said, choosing mates 'til death them did part. The old gander always sat real near his mate for protection through the month she sat on her eggs. We didn't dare go near, for there would be a fierce fight and many a hiss from the old fellow. I remember how we loved to search for goose eggs, they were so large. One time we had two old ganders that came at us tooth and toenail every time we went into the lot where they were kept. We were really afraid of them.

On Friday afternoons one of our teachers taught us to be great speechmakers, that we must each have a speech or poem ready for Friday afternoon. My sister was much distressed when Friday drew near and no poem. So Daddy said, "Oh, don't worry, I'll write one for you!" So he did:
"We have two old sturdy ganders
That I wish was over in Flanders,
For when I go to hunt the eggs
They flop and bite my legs.
And to holler 'tis no use
Dad won't come to pull them loose!"

Twice a year we were so pleased to get a few new store-bought clothes! Especially the neat little button shoes that took the place on Sundays of the tanned cow-hide ones we wore to school! How we did make them last until the next land-slide when we sold our wool or picked chestnuts to sell. We would go in the summer in our bare feet until we were nearly in sight of the church, carrying our precious shoes, then when we got near, we would put them on.

Perhaps here I should say something about our new log schoolhouse. It served us well for my first seventeen years. Many of the pupils went right on to school until they were twenty or more years of age, for there were no places of higher learning available at that time. It was before the days of coal, so we had a large stove that looked like a sawed-off log placed on its side, door at one end and a small hearth under it. Huge logs were sawed that kept the fire burning all day and we were sometimes more than comfortable if we sat near the roaring fire. It was quite a treat for the bigger boys to bring in another load of wood. Also it was a treat to go a quarter of a mile to a spring on a farm for water. We all drank from the same dipper. The bucket sat on the shelf along with our little tin pails where our dinners were placed. Dinner for many consisted of pieces of corn pone and a tin or cup of sorghum with butter. Just the same, we grew in stature and strength, and some in knowledge. We knew no such thing as paper and lead pencil, or they were too expensive, I don't know which. We had slates and slate pencils. They were a little hard to get. When one wore out or was used up, we'd crawl under the schoolhouse and search for a slate pencil that might have fallen through a crevice in the floor. That failing, there was a bank on the road some distance away where soap stones were to be found, so we could use those as makeshift pencils. We had big desks with shelves for our McGuffey books. We were allowed to sit two to a seat, which was quite a pleasure if, and when the teacher's back was turned, we could get in a little visiting on the sly. But we were going to school to study, which we did. We were supposed to know the entire multiplication table by heart by the time we were eight years of age. How often did I review those lines in the early morning before I got out of my snug bed, and how proud I was when I could say them forward, backward, inward, and outward! Then we memorized every poem in McGuffey's readers. I still get a thrill out of *The Old Oaken Bucket*, *The Blue and the Gray*, *The Inchcape Rock*, and many others. The last day of school we had to prepare plays, poems, and really get up and make a stagger, at least, of saying them. I was a bashful pupil, so what an ordeal to get up in front of what seemed like a thousand faces and say my piece.

Decorating the schoolhouse was, we thought, a masterpiece. We saved the newspapers through the winter so as to have enough for the older girls to cut out into lace curtains to cover part of the windows. Then we went to the creek for Spring Pine and every crack and crevice held a branch. There were contests all morning in spelling and arithmetic, in which some of our parents took part. How proud I was of my Daddy's education! How he could win contests! He knew math so well that everyone else seemed dumb to us.

Sugar-making time came in the early spring. My daddy spent many a winter hour making what we called spiles for the sap to seep through and drip into the troughs. The troughs were big and heavy and it took hard work to wash and clean them, carry and get them ready at the right time. Sometimes Dad would take me with him to sugar camp where I spent the night through when the big stir-off came. Then it was that we had to call on our Aunt Catherine who could make the cakes of sugar just right. Sometimes Mother would go along to help and that was a treat for me. I can almost see Dad yet as he hurried from task to task, lighting the big fires, placing spouts in place, and pouring, pouring troughs of sap into the ready barrels. He'd come whistling back to camp to fill the great iron kettles with the sweet sap. When it was boiling, the air all around was filled with the sweet fragrance! When twilight came, Daddy threw an armload of sheepskins under the lea of a great log near the camp and said, "Time for my girl to go to bed!" He tucked me in and I lay there just listening and wondering. The bright sparks from the burning logs mingled with the stars in the tops of the trees, they were so near. The frogs and the crickets must have loved that night as well as I, for they sang and chirped until I fell asleep, to the sounds of animals as they prowled the woods. I could hear the bark of a fox not far away, and the howl of a wildcat away down the hollow, and once that night I heard an owl who-whooing. I slept the whole night through but at early dawn Dad came over and woke me gently. "Lie real still," he told me, "I think there's some animal around nearby." But it just turned out to be a big old brown bear wanting a taste of our maple sugar. He was easily scared off.

Our parents saw to it that we had time for play away from our daily tasks. Father always took time off if our cousins came in the late afternoon, to have a romp with us all. If we played hide-and-seek it was hard to tell where Father would put us. And when we worked along with him in the fields, we had to watch out for some unusual prank from him. If we drank out of a stream or spring, we were sure to get a ducking, or our faces pushed into the water. But I don't think I ever had a switch or a paddle used on me.

Soon after our new house was built, when I was about eleven, some engineers came to board with us and Daddy became a member of the gang—a full-fledged engineer. He stayed with the job for forty-five years. We had come into a fortune. My Father earned (can you believe it!) forty-five dollars a month! After ten years this was raised to sixty dollars, and after another ten years, to eighty dollars, and by and by to one hundred dollars! Then, when there came the offer of another raise, he refused it, saying he wasn't worth that to the company.

My brother and I were left pretty much to ourselves after age ten, with a few jobs now and then like cutting the sandberries or the white daisies from a ten-acre field, or the bitterweeds out of a newly-cleared pasture. We had a good time roaming the woods and fields, hunting birds' nests, now and then burning out a hornets' nest. One day we came across our farm animals lying under a cluster of shade trees on the far brink of our hill. Before I could get my breath my brother, Owen, had jumped astride the neck of a big long horned steer. All the animals stampeded, led by that steer, their heels rattling, as with many a moo—moo—off they took to circle the hill. I cut across the near way and reached the slope just in time to see brother tumble off unhurt, perhaps not scared. All the animals were considerate and went around him. Also, we walked so many rail fences, climbed so many trees, got so many falls. We weren't afraid or perhaps we were both too young to know the danger.

All my life I think the death angel comes real near taking me. So I'll first tell of the few times in my youthful years. The first occurred when I wasn't more than four years of age and we still lived in our old log house. We only owned one horse, old Nell, and she was cross. I think she must have known she was imposed on, and wanted to get even some way. Mother had sent me to our old barrel spring for a small bucket of water, when old Nell, grazing nearby, saw me she came with ears back, teeth showing, and her fierce attack left me for dead when Mother and others reached me. I was hard to kill and it seems I still am. Then when I was several years older Mother took me along with her to gather huckleberries. When I climbed over a real large log, I landed plump right on a seven foot rattle snake. No use to say I wasn't frightened this time.

As he coiled like a spring, his head high in the air and his rattlers jingling, somehow I made it back onto the log soon enough to avoid his fatal strike. My third adventure happened when Mother thought I was old enough to milk a cow. This one, with her first calf, decided to show fight. When I entered the shed, she came at me with head lowered and would have left me pinned to the wall but as luck would have it (or maybe fate) I threw up my hands. The bucket caught over the long horn of the angry animal and while she was freeing herself for the second try, I was able to escape and close the door. That cow was never milked and soon ended in the butcher shop. My guardian angel came to my rescue.

Turning back pages and pages of time, leaves me thinking that along with the dangers came fierce storms and fierce spells of weather. Our winters set in early and hung on late. Sometimes we would not have a thaw for the entire winter. Our roads to school were drifted or clogged with snow almost throughout the school months. Sometimes Father could get through and take us to school in a sleigh which was all fun. Sometimes we had to walk or go horseback over the hills, and abandon our road for months. Other times the sun would peep out, the snow would melt a little, then another snow would come, until a crust was formed over which we could walk. The snow drifts were almost mountains, but we children loved this way of travel, rather than over the tops of wind-blown hills. We also had Jewish peddlers that came occasionally and gave us something to look forward to. It was almost like having Santa Claus come, even if Mother couldn't afford to buy much. We loved to see the big bundle opened up, for we seldom saw new things. I remember the Jewish peddler by name of Cohen, who got caught in a storm at our place and had to stay several days. Later I understand he was one of the founders of the Cohen Drug Stores. He certainly got his start the hard way.

Thinking of storms, a storm really had to be a fierce one or I enjoyed them. I especially liked those sudden thunderstorms with their streaks of bright lightning that came on hot spring or summer months. If a deep snow storm was in the process of making, our farm animals seemed to know ahead. Our old mother sow, you could see making her preparations by carrying hay, corn fodder, or whatever rubbish she could find and piling it all around her bed. Then when the storm struck she almost hibernated until the weather quieted down again. Also the barnyard fowls seemed to sense the coming of a storm. The geese huddled close together. The chickens would fly from place to place and into the air almost like they were drunk. But the best sign of all, when a real big storm was on the way, was our old Meadow River. For several days before a real storm broke it would seem to gather force and we could hear the loud roar. Mother would say, "This is going to be a bad storm I know by the way the river roars." The worst storm that I can recall lasted for more than a week. We knew all the signs and my dad began to make preparations. Plenty of big logs were piled on the porch, kindling wood of all sizes and kinds stacked behind our little flat topped kitchen stove. The windows were made secure, and hay was piled into the floor of the old barn on the hill. Then about all we could do was just sit and watch the bright fire and wait. School was called off for fear of falling trees. During the night we heard one big tree give up the ghost and crash to the ground.

Our barn set on top of the hill above the house, the first part of it to go as the wind swept across, were the two big doors. Father knew then that is was time to get the farm animals to a shed on the lea of the hill. Soon the wind snaked through and the shingles began to tumble from the roof of that old barn. Then hay came along with the shingles rolling in great bunches almost to the house. Glad we were to be snugly sheltered where we could watch the great logs in the fireplace send off their bright sparks and the little bright blazes. Sometimes we would climb to look out the high window and count the fallen trees as they looked much like a vandalized cemetery with all the stones toppled. We just waited out that storm almost holding our breath for fear our farm animals had suffered but they at least lived through but no doubt were much in need of food and water. When this long storm came, we still lived in our old staunch log house. I haven't mentioned our furniture in that house. First, and most, we had two immense sized beds. One in each corner of that big room. I do not remember about our chairs but I know we must have had some kind for I can recall cuddling against Mother's knees, scared about to death when some visitor was relating a ghost story. Underneath the big high beds we had what we called trundle beds, that could be pulled out for us children to sleep in when we had visitors. By and by Mother got a sewing machine then much later we afforded a bureau (now called a dresser). Of course, everyone had one of those big eight-day clocks with weights with its loud tick-tock. There in that big, dark room at night near the clock was where the ghosts stayed, that I feared so much. We had a little flat top stove, very small it seems, a homemade table to eat from, a bench along one side, shelves out of boards for our dishes, and cakes of maple sugar. Two barrels were in the corner for meal and flour. I quite well recall when Mother went to our little country store a few miles away and brought back the most wonderful piece of furniture, carrying it on her lap on old Nell. It was a box, maybe 8 inches in depth by 18 by 24 inches with two little drawers with these words written in gold color on each, "Clark, ONT. Spool Cotton." For sure we were rich. We had furniture. Then one day in the springtime when I had gone to the sugar camp with my daddy, I came home and lo and behold our dresser was all decked out with what I thought was masterpieces. In the form of J. Lynn catalogs taken and the leaves folded to the center and thus made a round globe: My sister had hatched up the idea. She was two years older than I. I couldn't have been prouder of her if she had constructed a velvet davenport for our living room. How I did wish I was smart like my sis. By and by we had to move into our new house, which was much more comfortable but no more lovable. That new house lived for about twenty-five or thirty years, then caught fire and burned down, leaving the stone chimney to which another and bigger house was built and is still standing. It is located overlooking a wonderful western view, a spot made especially for a house, but the view to me is dimmed, for so many of the ones I loved have passed to the great beyond.

So many farms in the distance which looked like checkerboards dotting the woods that surrounded them are gone. Now most of these farms consist of briers and brambles. A small creek ran its winding way in a hollow below our new house and deep along its bed were the tallest spruce pines that you can imagine. As I started on my way to school each morning, I stopped on the little stile at our gate to look at the tops of these tall pines seeming like giants, that often glistened with sleet or snow. That little creek made straight for the west until it emptied into our old Meadow River. In late afternoons it pointed toward the most wonderful western sunset that could be imagined. But when logging companies came in, they sure played hob with our hills and streams. Things were left tumbled in every direction, much worse than strip mining of today. Never again will our big pines show their plumes.

Compared with the handy gadgets of today our way of life was hard. Often my sis or I went to milk old Brindle (our cow) in the mid afternoon when the sun seemed so hot. This we did to have fresh cool milk for supper along with our hard earned corn bread. Mother would strain the milk, put it into a large pan, and place it to swim in the cold spring. We thought of nothing better.

There was a deep ice cold sulphur spring at the very farthest corner of the big pasture field. How often I now wonder did I make that long trip for a bucket of cold water when a visitor came calling. Or, how many, many buckets of water did we carry up that steep hill to the crew of men who harvested our hay. It kept my brother and me continually pacing up and down across fences for bucket after bucket of cold water for the men. We had one field that nature must have had a pick on. That was our steep hillside pasture field below the road, that dipped deep into the western woods. I can merely remember when Father cleared the first of that big field and when he plowed the ground with a yoke of oxen. He would once in a while allow me to ride above the plow-share between the handles that he held. I sometimes got a jerk but managed to stick on. Then when that field was planted into corn, the little striped chipmunks seemed to come from under every rock. Father made dead-fall traps for them and we children soon learned to search for the little dead pests and to reset the traps. Then we often had to go with pans and sticks, or bells and rattle, and pound around in the early morning, almost frozen, to frighten these little squirrels away—otherwise all Dad's labor would have been in vain. Even then, he had to plant corn over and over.

Diseases of epidemic forms often seemed to hit at intervals. Perhaps the one and only dipper used at school helped to spread some of the germs. They seemed to start in a small community about eight miles from where we lived, sometimes working their way nearer and nearer our home and leaving us much frightened. The first that I can clearly remember was a severe form of diptheria. It took about all the children in that little valley, and four out of five in a home in our own neighborhood. I think my Mother and Daddy expected the worst. I would hear them talking that three out of four children in one home was buried in the same grave. I think the weather was so cold on our hills that even germs could not exist so we caught no diptheria.

When later on an epidemic of spinal meningitis struck in this same location, that really scared me, as I heard how one patient after another had died an awful death, or perhaps worse, some

119

were left crippled for life. When typhoid fever came it was no respector of persons; old and young took it the same, here, there, and yonder. It was a terrible thing which I have no difficulty recalling. The doctors thought a drink of water or any form of food would kill an ill patient for certain, so the ill suffered so many ways. Their temperature went high, nothing to be given to lessen it. (Oh, I might say warm medicine.) How far has medical science gone since back then is a wonder to me. I forgot to say that typhoid took two of my very best school mates.

Here is about as good a place as any to tell you some of the hard ways we had to do things so long ago. No handy gadgets or tools.

About once a month two bushels of corn or wheat had to be taken to the old grist mill five miles away, or we would have no corn pones (perhaps no flour for biscuits). But to get that corn after it was raised, shucked, and dried ready for the mill was quite a task within itself. To make the job easier my dad and all farmers made themselves what they called pestles or some such name. They went to the hickory tree field and cut a large pole at least six inches through, then the whittling began, usually at night after a twelve or fifteen hours work shift on the farm. When finished, this pole was a broom stick except for one end which was peeled and left entire, but deep notches were cut into it. Now it was ready for use. Then Mother cleaned the floors; Dad brought into our living room his sacks of corn on the cob, an empty barrel with bottom and top off. Into this barrel he poured a part of his corn. Then he heaved that huge pole up and down, up and down, each lick shelling off some of the grain, then more corn and more pounding. If too much, the barrel was lifted onto a new place, with all the partly-shelled corn left on the floor and so the party went. As soon as the first ears of corn were out of the barrel each and all of us children knew to pitch in and shell corn for all we were worth until the job was done and someone was on the way to the old mill. The first time I was sent I did not know the way so I found myself lost traveling back toward home. I made the second try and the horse found the way for me. Then I got a thrill out of watching the grains of corn feed through the grinder, and the big stone wheel turn by the waters of a creek that emptied into our Meadow River.

It was just about as hard to get coffee ready for breakfast as it was to get a pone of cornbread. We couldn't buy roasted coffee, so we got the green grains. We had to be careful as we roasted it in our little flat topped wood stove. It was so easy to get it all scorched. So someone had to sit and watch and turn it from time to time. Then the first coffee grinder that I can recall was nailed to a post on the wall. It seemed to me it could only swallow one grain at a time as I so often had the job of grinding the coffee while my eight-year-old sister got breakfast. My father thought we should be brought up to work so he made Mother start us into the job early. Our kitchen was cold! Oh, so cold! The water in the buckets was always frozen over during the nighttime in winter. Our dish cloths were frozen stiff and I could add that by the time I got coffee enough fed through that little mill my feet were almost like ice. After all, Mother and Dad had the hard jobs. Father cleared land and not an hour could he afford to lose. Mother colored, knit, and spun linsey for our school clothes.

Sometimes Mother would bring from our two by four store a scrap of calico for a dress for my sister and me, but Mother did not like to sew. She started us in young. I think I made my first dress when I was ten years old.

John B. Nutter

My granddad passed away in June, 1893. His death left a vacant spot in my heart. No more errands along with him, no more sitting on his knee. As if listening to his good advice, his dog Watch knew he was not to follow Granddad and his big gray horse. So poor Watch came to his bedside a day or so before he left us, and placed his feet on the sick bed. Then and there he bade farewell to his master, Granddad Nutter. Granddad said (with his hand on old Watch's head) "Poor old Watch. I wonder what you will do, I'm leaving you." At that, Watch walked out the door with drooping head and came the one-half mile to our home. He never went back, but lived the rest of his days with us.

Here I bid my dear Granddad goodbye so I'll close this long story.

I think I always liked school and all my teachers but I had to be the tom boy both for my daddy and my granddaddy, so I was sometimes kept home from school to do chores for both in the fall of the year. About the first that I recall of helping my granddad was when they killed hogs. They called for me to carry water from the nearby spring to wash and clean everything but the squeal. I wasn't fond of the job, but the hardest thing was when the sorghum mill came along in the fall of the year. I rode the old slow horse round and round, turning the mill. Then before the job was over at my home, Granddad had his field of cane ready and nothing would do him but for me to ride again. I begged for my brother Owen to take the job but all said he was too slow. I was older and spry enough to apply the switch to old Nell, so I stayed from school.

My old Granddad was someone special to me. I loved to go along far back of his farm house to milk the half dozen cows. I couldn't help milk but we could talk. He told me many things I did not forget. He had a special spring house, with a stone floor, and a deep spring in the back part. But before he set the buckets of milk in the spring house, he poured a half dozen iron containers full of milk and called, "Kitty, kitty." The half dozen cats of all colors came in a run. He said he kept them to feed on the many mice and save his grain. My good old Granddad kept much money in gold hidden away, some in wheat bins. He also had orchards with every kind of fruit, apples of every flavor, and a big barn full of cattle. I had to hunt the eggs in a dozen places, climbing from one mow to another. My grandmother saw that I did the job well. She was harder on me than my granddad. She didn't know that little skinny legs

122

ever got tired.

When my daddy decided to take the job away from home (except on weekends), I thought the earth had fallen in on us. I had followed in his tracks over hills and meadows, up hill down hill, being his handyman, or tom boy and now it would be mostly up to me and my younger brother to look after the farm stock and the small chores. My sister could do the housekeeping, my mother the garden and milking. All went well with Owen and me through the summer. We had all the time we needed to slip off and loaf, but when the cold dark days of winter came, so did the story change also. How I did dread facing the icy wind, and going to the old barn on the hill a quarter of a mile, and do the feeding of the farm animals. The shocks of corn fodder were frozen. The hay was frozen. Our toes and fingers were frozen. This was an early morning task before school time, but when spring came I really liked to care for the ewes and new lambs. I think I grew to be the shepherd of the family. I never forgot to put the sheep into their fold (or shed) where no fox could get in to carry off a lamb, and I always found a lamb I could take to the house to pet before the season was over. Also, I was given a calf for my own to pet. I haven't forgotten the Sunday I forgot to feed my calf and went to church with the family. In church I thought of my calf. How I wished for that preacher to cut his sermon short. The very minute he said, "Amen," I hit it like a streak, down the hill, I never stopped running. I was merely hoping I'd find my calf alive, if only breathing. I grabbed my feed as I ran, and when I opened the door, lo and behold a live but hungry calf. I never forgot after this. I felt like singing hallelujah.

My granddad's farm buildings were large and rambly. The house within a house, the barn, a barn within a barn. The barn was divided into two parts, exactly alike, with a wide solid puncheon floor between. I had to search for hen eggs east and west. Sometimes, maybe for adventure, maybe to save time and get home earlier, I would climb up high over the floor, right into the comb of the roof, and would hold by my hands to cracks between the big logs, and with my feet placed the same way as I slipped across from one side of the big barn to the other side. What a risk! If my feet or my hands had slipped, they would have found only a big splash, some 30 feet below, with pockets full of broken eggs thrown in. All this climbing and trips from one place to another made my muscles as strong as whipcord. Maybe that's why they lasted one hundred years.

I shall never forget the one dark night soon after my granddad died when my dad asked me if I could go up to the old empty house and get some medicine for my grandmother, who had moved in with us, and was having some kind of attack. I thought well, I'll try at least. The road was dark. Trees lined each side. Sometimes a wildcat would run through the brush back then, so I was scared, really scared, but nothing compared to the way I felt when I opened the door of that big dark house. I felt my way to the mantle, and grabbed the bottles. The cold chills ran up my spine. I was sure ghostly hands were reaching out to embrace me. I could distinctly feel them. Oh, those many big dark rooms! I was so glad to get outside that I ran the one-half mile home never thinking of the shadowy road. That was one frightening experience for me.

When I was 14 years of age, that big old rambly house haunted me for years after this. I would have nightmares of ghosts prowling about, but when Dad and Mother moved into it in the year 1909, this all changed. No more ghosts.

After I went to teaching, I loved to go to Summersville, in Nicholas County, and attend what we called Teachers' Institute. I always met some new and some old friends. We exchanged ideas with each other and were given instruction at the Institute on how to become better teachers.

Times were changing. A new school building had been built near the old log school house. It was covered with wood siding and painted white. How happy I was to teach in this new building. I loved teaching and seeing children learn. The school building still stands today but is no longer in use since consolidated schools have come into being.

The new house, which was built after our old one burned, has been improved and partly remodeled. It now belongs to my son and is often used as a meeting place for family members, who have settled here, there, and yonder. The land is used for a Christmas tree farm. No longer does the old barn stand, but it is not needed since there are no animals to use it. The big yard is kept neatly trimmed and fenced.

I have enjoyed going back to the old home place and being able to remember days gone by and to have my children and grandchildren meet for a family get-together. Now, I am no longer able to travel back home as I used to do. As I said before, "Times have changed," but so have I.